Animal Rights

by Karen D. Povey

LUCENT BOOKS
A part of Gale, Cengage Learning

Detroit • New York • San Francisco • New Haven, Conn • Waterville, Maine • London

© 2009 Gale, Cengage Learning

ALL RIGHTS RESERVED. No part of this work covered by the copyright herein may be reproduced, transmitted, stored, or used in any form or by any means graphic, electronic, or mechanical, including but not limited to photocopying, recording, scanning, digitizing, taping, Web distribution, information networks, or information storage and retrieval systems, except as permitted under Section 107 or 108 of the 1976 United States Copyright Act, without the prior written permission of the publisher.

Every effort has been made to trace the owners of copyrighted material.

LIBRARY OF CONGRESS CATALOGING-IN-PUBLICATION DATA

Povey, Karen D., 1962–
  Animal rights / by Karen D. Povey.
    p. cm. — (Hot topics)
  Includes bibliographical references and index.
  ISBN 978-1-4205-0079-0 (hardcover)
  1. Animal rights. I. Title.
  HV4711.P68 2008
  179'.3—dc22

2008018283

Lucent Books
27500 Drake Rd.
Farmington Hills, MI 48331

ISBN-13: 978-1-4205-0079-0
ISBN-10: 1-4205-0079-1

Printed in the United States of America
1 2 3 4 5 6 7 13 12 11 10 09

CONTENTS

FOREWORD	**4**
INTRODUCTION	**6**
The Role of Animals	
CHAPTER ONE	**9**
Should Animals Have Rights?	
CHAPTER TWO	**25**
Farming Animals for Food	
CHAPTER THREE	**40**
Animal Experimentation	
CHAPTER FOUR	**57**
Animals in Sport and Entertainment	
CHAPTER FIVE	**74**
Animal Rights and Wildlife	
CHAPTER SIX	**91**
The Tactics of Animal Rights Activists: Do They Go Too Far?	
NOTES	**106**
DISCUSSION QUESTIONS	**111**
ORGANIZATIONS TO CONTACT	**113**
FOR MORE INFORMATION	**115**
INDEX	**117**
PICTURE CREDITS	**120**
ABOUT THE AUTHOR	**120**

FOREWORD

Young people today are bombarded with information. Aside from traditional sources such as newspapers, television, and the radio, they are inundated with a nearly continuous stream of data from electronic media. They send and receive e-mails and instant messages, read and write online "blogs," participate in chat rooms and forums, and surf the Web for hours. This trend is likely to continue. As Patricia Senn Breivik, the former dean of university libraries at Wayne State University in Detroit, has stated, "Information overload will only increase in the future. By 2020, for example, the available body of information is expected to double every 73 days! How will these students find the information they need in this coming tidal wave of information?"

Ironically, this overabundance of information can actually impede efforts to understand complex issues. Whether the topic is abortion, the death penalty, gay rights, or obesity, the deluge of fact and opinion that floods the print and electronic media is overwhelming. The news media report the results of polls and studies that contradict one another. Cable news shows, talk radio programs, and newspaper editorials promote narrow viewpoints and omit facts that challenge their own political biases. The World Wide Web is an electronic minefield where legitimate scholars compete with the postings of ordinary citizens who may or may not be well informed or capable of reasoned argument. At times, strongly worded testimonials and opinion pieces both in print and electronic media are presented as factual accounts.

Conflicting quotes and statistics can confuse even the most diligent researchers. A good example of this is the question of whether or not the death penalty deters crime. For instance, one study found that murders decreased by nearly one-third when the death penalty was reinstated in New York in 1995. Death penalty supporters cite this finding to support their argument that the existence of the death penalty deters criminals from committing murder. However, another study found that states without the death penalty have murder rates below the national average. This study is cited by opponents of capital punishment, who reject the claim that the death penalty deters murder. Students need context and clear, informed discussion if they are to think critically and make informed decisions.

The Hot Topics series is designed to help young people wade through the glut of fact, opinion, and rhetoric so that they can think critically about controversial issues. Only by reading and thinking critically will they be able to formulate a viewpoint that is not simply the parroted views of others. Each volume of the series focuses on one of today's most pressing social issues and provides a balanced overview of the topic. Carefully crafted narrative, fully documented primary and secondary source quotes, informative sidebars, and study questions all provide excellent starting points for research and discussion. Full-color photographs and charts enhance all volumes in the series. With its many useful features, the Hot Topics series is a valuable resource for young people struggling to understand the pressing issues of the modern era.

INTRODUCTION

THE ROLE OF ANIMALS

Humans have a long history of association with animals. Prehistoric hunter-gatherers captured and ate animals even before they learned to fashion hunting weapons or discovered fire for cooking meat. Thousands of years ago, humans began domesticating animals, creating creatures docile enough for living close to people and serving as food animals, beasts of burden, and guardians.

For most of history, people viewed animals as property, useful only for providing food, clothing, and labor. Even today, some people still support this viewpoint, arguing that animals were created for the sole use of humans as written in the Bible: "And God said, Let us make man in our image, after our likeness; and let them have dominion over the fish of the sea, and over the fowl of the air, and over the cattle, and over all the earth, and over every creeping thing that creepeth upon the earth." (Gen. 1:24–26)

Eventually, however, as people began moving off farms and into cities, some animals, such as dogs and cats, became less necessary for work and were given new roles as household companions. Today, in many regions of the world, animals have been elevated to cherished members of the family, with people spending large amounts of money to ensure the well-being of their pets.

As the role of animals in society evolved, people's attitudes regarding the treatment of animals also changed. In the early 1800s, some people began to take notice of the suffering of animals used by people and started questioning their often cruel treatment. One of the first people to propose the idea that animals deserved consideration as something more than just human property was the Reverend Humphrey Primatt, who expressed his views in Britain in 1776. He wrote, "See that no brute of any kind . . . whether intrusted to thy care, or coming in thy way, suffer thy neglect or abuse. Let no views of profit, no compliance with custom, and no fear of ridicule of the world, ever tempt thee to the least act of cruelty or injustice to any creature whatsoever."[1]

This plea for compassion toward animals has gained a significant following in recent times. The campaign to improve people's treatment of animals has become a widely accepted movement. Animal activists have begun to question even the most traditional uses of animals for food or sport. Proponents

The campaign to improve society's treatment of animals has now become a worldwide movement.

of animal rights insist that animals deserve to be treated as more than mere "things" and object to any uses that sacrifice their well-being to benefit humans.

Animal rights advocates challenge the long-held belief that animals are resources to be hunted, eaten, and used for clothing or labor. The methods used by animal rights organizations to promote this viewpoint are often controversial and sometimes even illegal. In many cases, however, their efforts have been successful. The last few decades have brought many new animal protection laws and improved conditions for animals used in agriculture and medical research.

There still remains a huge gap between the views of animal rights activists and those who accept the use of animals, however. While most people embrace the idea of eliminating cruelty toward animals and improving their treatment, many fewer support the animal rights activists' goal to end animal use completely.

SHOULD ANIMALS HAVE RIGHTS?

Currently, most people do not think of animals as having rights. People can own animals, making them property. People can raise, slaughter, and eat farm animals. People can confine animals to cages and use them for research or display them in zoos. People can force animals to compete in sports such as dog racing and rodeos. People can track, kill, and exhibit trophies of wild animals. Although people are able to use and control animals in many ways, there are numerous laws in place to govern these activities. These laws were established to prevent the mistreatment of animals by people.

WHY ARE DIFFERENCES IMPORTANT?

"Maybe it is easier to harm other animals if we distance ourselves from them—we are so different from other animals, we tell ourselves, that it is all right to harm them." —Mark Bekoff, professor and author of many books on animal behavior and emotions.

Strolling with Our Kin. Jenkintown, PA: Anti-Vivisection Society, 2000, p. 15.

One of the earliest steps in promoting the humane treatment of animals was the creation of the Society for the Prevention of Cruelty to Animals (SPCA) in London in the 1820s. The formation of the American Society for the Prevention of Cruelty to Animals (ASPCA) followed in New York in 1866. The goal of these organizations was to bring attention to the suffering of animals at the hands of people. By the late 1800s, several other organizations were founded in the United States to campaign against animal cruelty. These groups helped create some of the first anticruelty laws designed to protect animals from harsh treatment and neglect.

One of the first of these laws was passed in New York in 1867. The provisions of the law were significant, because they demonstrated that although animals were legal property, they must be treated with concern and cared for under humane guidelines. The law created penalties for abusing animals, keeping animals for fighting, transporting animals in a cruel manner, and abandoning old or sick animals. Within a few years similar laws were enacted in many other states.

Current laws vary among states. Most address meeting an animal's basic needs by providing food, water, shelter, and medi-

The director of animal research at Rockefeller University in New York conducts a tour of the mice lab. Animal rights supporters argue that the unnecessary suffering of animals at the hands of people cannot be justified for any reason.

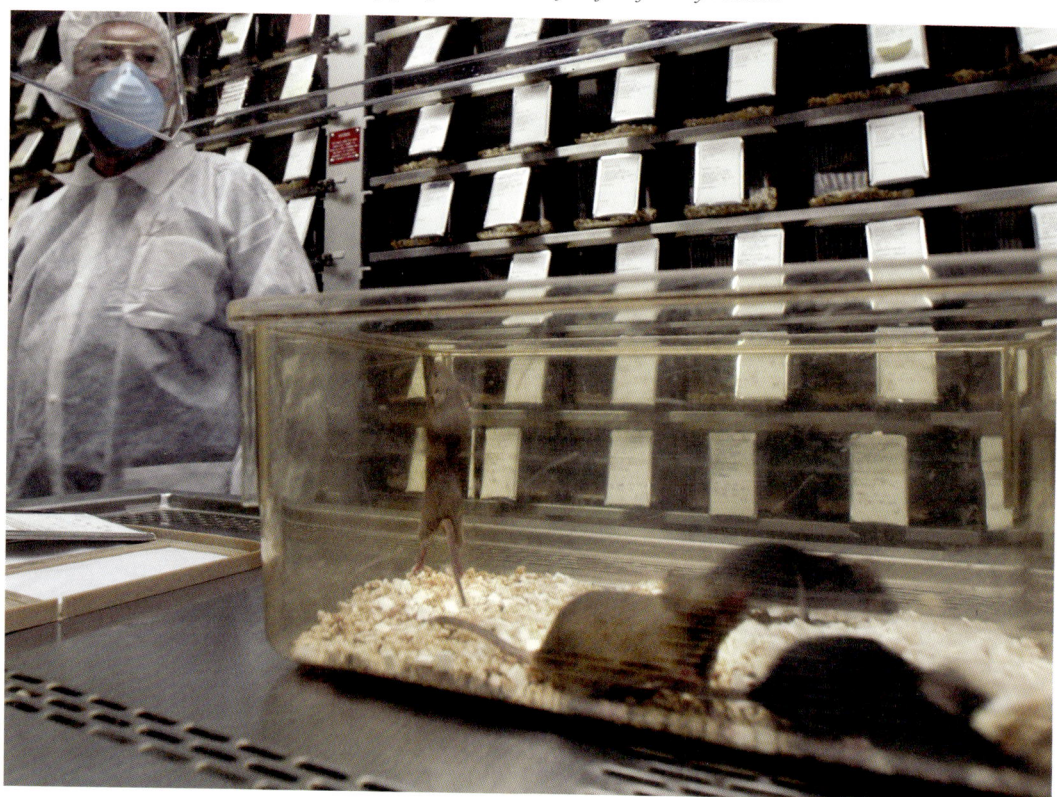

cal attention. Others cover specialized topics such as prohibiting the use of chicks and rabbits as contest prizes (California), regulating the confinement of pregnant pigs (Florida), and requiring that dogs be fitted with collars bearing identification tags (Rhode Island). Many laws now also govern the hunting or harassment of wild animals.

Animal Welfare or Animal Rights?

Animal welfare laws aim to eliminate the unnecessary suffering of animals that are used for purposes considered necessary to people. Generally, these purposes are evaluated based on the benefit they provide people. If human interests can be served through the use of an animal, then that purpose is considered necessary. For example, it is generally considered acceptable to kill animals for food or use them for medical research, because those purposes benefit people. Animal welfare laws ensure that animals used in this manner are provided with the best lives possible, given their circumstances. People concerned with animal welfare agree that animals should not be made to suffer unnecessarily to benefit people.

From Slave to Equal

"Animals, whom we have made our slaves, we do not like to consider our equal." —Charles Darwin, noted English naturalist who described the process of evolution.

Quoted in James Serpell, *In the Company of Animals*. New York: Basil Blackwell, 1986, p. 150.

Animal welfare is not the same thing as animal rights. People who work on animal welfare issues use science to determine ways to humanely care for animals. The animal rights movement, however, is based on an overall belief system. Supporters of animal rights oppose the idea of measuring the value of an animal's life in terms of its benefit to people. This mindset, they believe, reinforces the idea that animals are simply property. Instead of focusing on the treatment of animals, some people feel the real question should be whether the use of animals by

The Great Ape Project

The great apes—gorillas, chimpanzees, bonobos, and orangutans—share a close genetic relationship with humans. They also demonstrate many humanlike traits, such as distinct personalities, a high degree of intelligence, and the ability to form strong emotional attachments. These characteristics inspire many people to have strong feelings of kinship with apes and express concern over the way apes are exploited by people.

To protect great apes from use in medical research, the entertainment industry, or other activities that benefit humans, a group of animal rights activists founded the Great Ape Project in 1993.

The controversial goal of the Great Ape Project is to have the United Nations declare that these animals be granted the same basic rights as humans: the right to life, the right to individual liberty, and the prohibition of torture. This designation would mean that apes could no longer be viewed as property that could be owned and used for human benefit. Critics of the Great Ape Project's goal argue that shared DNA is not enough to grant human rights to apes. Without a moral sense of right and wrong to drive responsible behavior, apes are not deserving of the same rights as people. The real goal, many people argue, should be minimizing the suffering of apes simply because they suffer, not because they are so similar to humans.

The great apes share genetic traits, as well as many personality traits, with humans, which inspires many people to have strong feelings of kinship with apes.

people can be justified at all. Trying to balance human interests with those of animals is unrealistic, they believe, because human interests will always win out. Gary Francione, a noted professor of animal rights law, explains:

> The human property interest will almost always prevail. The animal in question is always a "pet" or a "laboratory" animal, or a "game" animal, or a "food" animal, or a "rodeo" animal, or some other form of animal property that exists solely for our use and has no value except as a means to our ends. There is really no choice to be made between the human and the animal interest because the choice has already been predetermined by the property status of the animal.[2]

For this reason Francione advocates a whole new way of looking at animals. Instead of considering them as property owned by people— as is the case in virtually all societies—he believes in applying "the principle of equal consideration." This principle proposes that the interests of animals should count as much as the interests of people. This does not mean that animals should have all the same rights as people. Granting animals freedom of speech or the right to vote would obviously make no sense. To Francione, equal consideration means that "we must extend to animals the one basic right that we extend to all human beings: the right not to be treated as things."[3] Using this principle, instead of applying animal welfare laws to govern the size of the cages used to house egg-laying chickens, an animal rights supporter would propose doing away with chicken farms entirely, because using chickens for egg-laying violates their right not to be used as a human resource. Most animal rights supporters believe that it is never necessary to harm or kill animals to benefit people.

What Differences Make a Difference?

The idea that animals deserve the same considerations as people gained a growing following in the 1970s, leading to the birth of the modern animal rights movement. At that time people began to question why animals should be considered inferior to humans. To answer this question, they looked for qualities that separate people and animals. One quality they considered was the use of language. While no animals use human language, scientific studies have discovered that many animals do use complex languages for communicating with others of their kind. Another area in which humans were once thought to be superior to

ANDi, the first genetically modified rhesus monkey, is shown in 2001. Scientific studies have found that many animals use complex languages for communicating with others of their kind, indicating intelligence.

animals was in the use of tools. However, it is now well-known that many animals use and even make tools.

One argument often made to separate people from animals is that people have greater intelligence and the ability to reason. However, long-term studies of animals such as chimpanzees and elephants have revealed startling insights into the abilities of animals to think in complex ways, including counting, planning for the future, deceiving others, and adjusting their behavior to new situations. This complex behavior makes it difficult to dismiss the idea that some animals possess intelligence and the ability to reason.

In addition, not all humans are smarter than animals. Although intelligence varies widely among species and individuals, animals are smart enough to survive in the situations for which they are adapted. If people were measured by animal standards, author Mark Bekoff believes, humans would likely fall short. "There are no animals who can program computers or practice law," he says. "But there are no humans who can fly like birds, swim like fish, run as fast as cheetahs, or carry as much weight—relative to their own body weight—as ants. So are humans unique? Yes, but so are all other animals. The important point that needs much discussion focuses on the question '*what differences make a difference?*'"[4]

The Capacity for Suffering

Animal rights supporters argue that the tests of language, tool use, and intelligence fail to provide evidence of great enough differences between animals and people to justify human superiority. Instead of looking for reasons to defend harming animals, they prefer pointing to reasons why animals should be entitled to the same protection from harm as people. Their argument is based on the issue of morality, or how people treat others. "Humane treatment of animals is first and foremost a moral issue; it concerns how humans *ought* to behave toward animals,"[5] says Francione. Although animal rights proponents acknowledge there are clear differences between animals and people, they point out that animals share one overriding similarity with people—the ability to suffer.

The capacity of animals to suffer is the key argument made for granting animals rights. In 1970 Richard Ryder coined the term *speciesism* to describe the practice of hurting others simply because they belong to a different species. Speciesism, Ryder believed, was a form of discrimination on a par with racism and sexism and was morally wrong. Ryder and other animal rights proponents believe that it is morally wrong to cause an animal to suffer for any reason, even if that animal's suffering would benefit people. To them, the suffering of an animal should be considered the same as human suffering. "We can treat different species differently, but always we should treat equal suffering equally,"[6] Ryder says.

Hard to Accept

"Common sense suggests that the overwhelming majority of Americans—and indeed of the world's population—will never accept the premise that it is wrong to humanely use animals." —Daniel T. Oliver, author and critic of the animal rights movement.

Daniel T. Oliver, *Animal Rights: The Inhumane Crusade.* Bellevue, WA: Merril Press, 1999, p. 132.

How does one evaluate animal suffering? Part of the answer lies with an animal's ability to feel pain. At one time many people thought that animals were merely living beings, unable to think or feel pain like people do. Today, however, most people recognize that certain animals react to pain by crying out or trying to flee, just as people do. Biologically, people have much in common with many animals, such as birds and mammals. Because they possess similar nervous systems, one might conclude that humans and animals process pain in a similar fashion. Less is understood about the ways that "lower" animals such as fish or invertebrates feel pain.

Animal Consciousness and Emotion

Even if animals do feel pain, is their experience the same as human pain? Certainly what is painful to one animal may not nec-

Should Animals Have Rights? 17

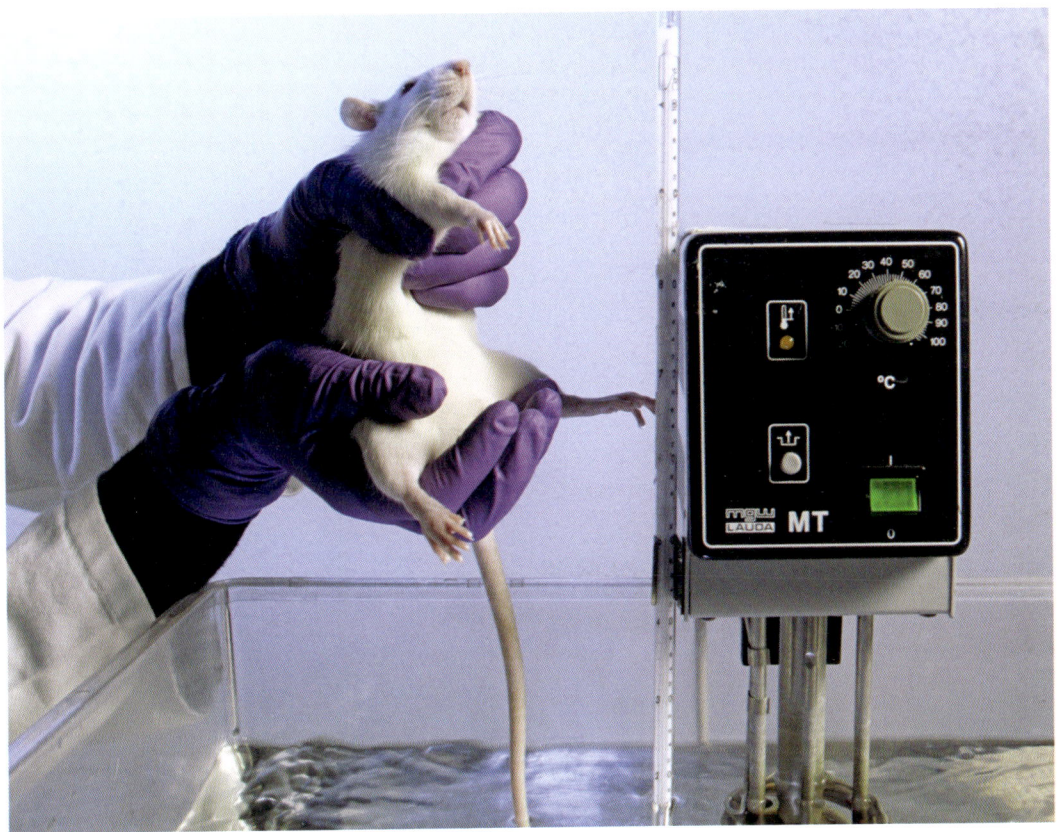

A scientist tests the pain tolerance of a rat by placing its tail in water heated to 39 degrees Celsius (102.2 degrees Fahrenheit). Many animal rights proponents believe that causing animals to suffer is morally wrong.

essarily be painful to another. For example, a horse would barely feel a slap that might be deadly to a mouse. When does the feeling of pain become suffering? Can suffering occur without physical pain, such as suffering from fear or anxiety?

For some people the answers lie in whether or not animals have an awareness of themselves and their place in the world. This awareness is called consciousness. People who oppose granting rights to animals argue that human consciousness far surpasses that of animals. "Some animals (cats and dogs) clearly think. But only humans think about thinking,"[7] explains L. Neil Smith. Unlike animals, humans use their consciousness to create purpose to their lives and appreciate its value and quality. As

> ### THEY ARE LIKE US
>
> "Like us, these animals are in the world, aware of the world, and aware of what happens to them. And, like us, what happens to these animals matters to them, whether anyone else cares about this or not." —Tom Regan, philosopher and proponent of animal rights.
>
> Quoted in Lisa Kemmerer, "Empty Cages: Facing the Challenge of Animal Rights," *Human Rights Quarterly*, February, 2007, p. 4.

a result, it is argued that animals' lives can never equal those of humans. "The fullest chicken life there has ever been, so science suggests, does not approach the full life of a human; the differences in capacities are just too great,"[8] insists philosopher R.G. Frey. Author Stephen Budiansky agrees:

> Our ability to have thoughts about our experiences turns emotions into something far greater and sometimes far worse than mere pain. . . . Sadness, pity, sympathy, condolence, self-pity, ennui, woe, heartbreak, distress, worry, apprehension, dejection, grief, wistfulness, pensiveness, mournfulness, brooding, rue, regret, misery, despair—all express shades of the pain of sadness whose full meaning comes only from our ability to reflect on their meaning, not just their feeling. . . . Consciousness is a wonderful gift and a wonderful curse that, all the evidence suggests, is not in the realm of the sentient experiences of other creatures.[9]

While it may be impossible to evaluate the degree to which animals are conscious, that question is irrelevant to most animal rights activists. Bekoff agrees that understanding animal consciousness has value, but he argues that "well-being centers on what animals feel, not what they know."[10] In his view, a cow doesn't need to understand its purpose in life to experience suffering. "Human self-awareness may be different, but 'different' does not necessarily translate into 'better' in any moral sense,"[11] argues Francione.

In fact, in some instances animals may show greater consciousness than some people. Author and animal rights leader Peter Singer explains:

> A chimpanzee, dog, or pig, for instance, will have a higher degree of self-awareness and a greater capacity for meaningful relations with others than a severely retarded infant or someone in a state of advanced senility. So if we base the right to life on these characteristics we must grant these animals a right to life as good as, or better than, such retarded or senile humans.[12]

Noted primate expert Jane Goodall is an outspoken advocate for animal rights and has an explanation for why some people

Chimpanzee expert Jane Goodall is an outspoken advocate for animal rights.

hold the view that animals lack any degree of consciousness: "It is easier to do unpleasant things to unfeeling objects—to subject them to painful experiments, raise them in intensive factory farms, and hunt, trap, eat, and otherwise exploit them—than it is to do these things to sapient, sentient beings. Fear in a monkey, a dog, or a pig being is probably experienced in much the same way as it is in a human being."[13]

The Morality of Animal Rights

Many people concerned with the welfare of animals readily admit that animals can think, feel emotions, and suffer if mistreated. They also believe that animals have basic biological rights, such as the ability to find food, water, and shelter and to reproduce. However, they disagree with the idea of providing rights to animals for moral reasons. "Because only humans are capable of moral and ethical behavior, only humans would have moral and ethical rights,"[14] explains animal sciences professor Leland Shapiro. Nature is often cruel; a lion makes no moral judgment about killing a gazelle, and housecats often toy with their injured prey before killing it. "One cannot assign moral rights to an individual who does not have moral responsibilities,"[15] says Shapiro.

Avoiding Speciesism

"To avoid speciesism we must allow that beings who are similar in all relevant respects have a similar right to life—and mere membership in our own biological species cannot be a morally relevant criterion for this right." —Peter Singer, philosopher whose book *Animal Liberation* significantly influenced the formation of the modern animal rights movement.

Peter Singer, *Animal Liberation*. New York: New York Review, 1975, p. 19.

In fact some people consider it immoral to consider animals equal to humans. University of Chicago law professor Richard Epstein explains:

> We have quite enough difficulty in persuading or coercing human beings to respect the rights of their fellows,

America's Most Humane Places

In 2007 the Humane Society of the United States (HSUS) inaugurated its Humane Index, a system that ranks the United States' twenty-five largest metropolitan areas according to their compassion for animals. Factors considered in the ranking process included the care of farm animals, media coverage of animal issues, and number of puppy-mill supporting pet stores, fur stores, wildlife care centers, and vegetarian restaurants. Top honors went to San Francisco, Seattle, Portland, Washington, D.C., and San Diego. At the bottom of the list were Chicago, Cincinnati, and Dallas.

The HSUS developed the Humane Index to determine how America's largest metro areas—representing 40 percent of the U.S. population—rank in terms of animal protection issues. According to the HSUS's Jennifer Fearing, "The Humane Index is a tool that helps people take action to improve the treatment of animals. In future years we hope to expand the Humane Index to include more cities and we encourage everyone to do what they can to make sure their community comes out on top next time around."

so that all can live in peace. By treating animals as our moral equals, we would undermine the liberty and dignity of human beings—making the slaughters of [Adolf] Hitler, [Joseph] Stalin, or Pol Pot seem no worse than the daily activity of preparing cattle for market. That is one kind of moral equivalence we must never allow. Animals are properly property. To misunderstand the rights of animals is to cheapen the rights of human beings.[16]

The Animal Rights Movement

Many people are concerned about the treatment of animals. Over four hundred organizations exist in the United States to promote animal welfare and animal rights. These organizations hold a wide variety of viewpoints regarding the use of animals. Traditional humane organizations seek to prevent animal cruelty and to improve treatment of animals, especially pets. Other welfare groups advocate improving the lives of animals used in laboratories or raised for food. The most vocal animal rights

People for the Ethical Treatment of Animals (PETA) is one of the world's largest animal rights groups. Here, a PETA activist protests the treatment of chickens by the KFC food chain.

organizations, however, present much stronger messages and often employ aggressive methods to reach their goals. One of the largest animal rights groups is People for the Ethical Treatment of Animals (PETA), claiming nearly 1.8 million members and supporters. PETA's many programs include campaigns against the livestock and fur industries, the use of animals for research, and the use of animals for entertainment.

Many animal rights organizations have goals similar to those stated by activist Tom Regan. "It is not larger, cleaner cages that justice demands, . . ." he says "but empty cages; not 'traditional' animal agriculture, but a complete end to all commerce in the flesh of dead animals; not 'more humane' hunting and trapping, but the total eradication of these barbarous practices."[17]

A Range of Concerns for Animals

Because some animal rights organizations do not openly express their goals in this manner, many of their members do not realize they are supporting campaigns to end the use of animals by people. In a 2003 Gallup poll, some people who stated their support for giving animals the same rights as people also stated that they opposed bans on medical testing of animals and tighter laws protecting farm animals. Many people also stated a preference for giving moral consideration to dogs and cats but not chickens or rats. These results demonstrate the public's widespread confusion about the difference between animal welfare and animal rights. Although many people claim to support animal rights, in reality many have views supporting animal welfare instead.

Animal Rights Law

Law schools throughout the United States are racing to meet the rapidly increasing demand for courses relating to animal rights and animal welfare. The number of such courses rose from nine in 2000 to eighty-six in 2007. Courses cover a variety of topics ranging from anticruelty laws to pet ownership issues and may eventually give rise to changes in the way the law views animals. These courses have been developed in response to growing numbers of lawsuits challenging the legal status of animals as property. In addition, lawyers are increasingly asked to assist with pet-custody issues in divorces, providing for pets in wills, and bringing lawsuits against mistakes made by veterinarians.

Many of these animal law courses are taught in some of the country's most prestigious universities, including Harvard Law School, Columbia Law School, Stanford Law School, and the University of California, Los Angeles, School of Law. Some of the funding for these courses comes from a foundation started by noted animal rights supporter Bob Barker, longtime host of the television game show *The Price Is Right*. Barker has provided $7 million in grants to support animal law courses since 2001.

Many people are concerned about the well-being of animals. At one end of the spectrum are people who embrace the philosophy of animal rights. At the other end are people who believe animals should have no rights at all. Most people have viewpoints that fall somewhere between these two extremes. Some people may oppose keeping farm animals in certain conditions but have no moral opposition to eating meat. Others may accept the use of rats and mice in medical research but oppose using primates for that purpose.

In Ryder's view, "Basically, it boils down to cold logic. If we are going to care about the suffering of other humans, then logically we should care about the suffering of non-humans too.... We all, thank goodness, feel a natural spark of sympathy for the sufferings of others. We need to catch that spark and fan it into a fire of rational and universal compassion."[18]

Farming Animals for Food

The vast majority of animals used by people are the farm animals that serve as a source of food and other products, such as leather and fur. In the United States, where meat and dairy products are considered staples of a nutritious diet, over 9 billion animals are killed each year for food. Billions more are killed worldwide. Americans consume over 200 pounds (91kg) of meat a year from livestock such as cattle, pigs, chickens, and turkeys.

Asking "Why?"

"The interesting question is not whether the cow should be able to sue the farmer for cruel treatment, but why the cow is there in the first place." —Gary Francione, law professor and animal rights advocate.

Gary Francione, "One Right for All," *New Scientist*, vol. 188, issue 2520, October 8, 2005, p. 24.

In order to provide enough meat at costs affordable to consumers, most food animals are raised on large "factory" farms where thousands of animals are kept in close confinement, often with little space to move freely or behave naturally. Animal rights activists raise many concerns about the treatment and condition of animals raised to satisfy America's demand for meat. People within the agriculture industry respond that consumer demand drives production methods, but they admit that they "need to continue to find methods of producing cheap and abundant foods without severely compromising the welfare of the animals being raised for that food production."[19]

Moral Schizophrenia?

Most people give little thought to the process that brings food from the farm to the dinner table. People purchase meat in the grocery store in tidy packages that bear little resemblance to the living animal it came from, making it easy for most to ignore the reality of meat production. This tendency troubles critics of the animal agriculture industry who are working to bring more attention to the facts of factory farming.

Animal rights supporters believe that people in industrialized societies such as the United States, Europe, and Australia

Most people give little thought to the process that brings food from the farm to the dinner table and ignore the reality of meat production.

exhibit a double standard in their concern for animals. People in these regions often express great concern for animal welfare, lavish large amounts of money on companion animals such as dogs and cats, and voice distress when pets are mistreated. However, most of them shrug off the plight of animals raised for food.

For Petting, Not Killing

"Animals are for petting, not killing. Meat, unrelated, is for eating. And never the twain shall meet." —Paul Vitello, writer for the *New York Times*.

Paul Vitello, "Being Nice to the Bacon, Before You Bring it Home," *New York Times*, April 1, 2007, p. 4.

Author and professor Richard Bulliet, an expert in the role of animals in human society, describes this trend:

> People live far away, both physically and psychologically, from the animals that produce the food, fiber, and hides they depend on, and they never witness the births, sexual congress, and slaughter of these animals. Yet they maintain very close relationships with companion animals—pets—often relating to them as if they were human.... [Society's] members experience feelings of guilt, shame, and disgust when they think (as seldom as possible) about the industrial processes by which domestic animals are rendered into products and about how those products come to market.... Meat, leather, and test animals are hard to give up, but details about what goes on behind the scenes to provide these goods and cultural services are revolting. Pets and wildlife evoke deep positive feelings, but domestic animals feeding the consumer market are a morally troubling reality.[20]

Author Gary Francione coined the term "moral schizophrenia" to describe the double standard people seem to apply to pets and food animals. He says, "We may be said to suffer from a sort of 'moral schizophrenia' when it comes to our thinking about animals. We claim to regard animals as having morally significant interest, but we treat them in ways that belie our claims."[21] As an example of this contradiction, James Serpell, author of *In the Company of Animals*, compares society's treatment of pets and pigs. He describes the natural intelligence of pigs, their clean and social nature, and their ability to form strong bonds with people who raise them from piglets. In addition, pigs provide people with a wide range of useful products from food to leather. In contrast, the millions of cats, dogs, birds, and fish kept as pets provide no useful purpose beyond companionship. According to Serpell:

> Here then is the paradox. At one extreme are the animals we call pets. They make little or no practical or economic contribution to human society, yet we nurture and care for them like our own kith and kin, and display outrage and disgust when they are subjected to ill-treatment. At the other, we have animals like the pig on which a major section of our economy depends; supremely useful animals in every respect. . . . And in return for this outstanding contribution, we treat pigs like worthless objects devoid of feelings and sensations. By rights, we ought to be eternally grateful to pigs for the extraordinary sacrifices they make on our behalf. Instead, the quality of life we impose on them suggests nothing but contempt and hatred.[22]

Modern Animal Agriculture

The poor quality of life that Serpell refers to is a reflection of the goals of the modern animal agriculture industry. Today the goal of animal agriculture is to produce the greatest amount of meat at the lowest possible cost. Animal scientists have increased production through the development of feeds that cause animals to grow more rapidly or produce more eggs and milk. Animals are also selectively bred to create creatures that have leaner meat or other characteristics popular with consumers.

The main way the industry increases production while keeping costs down is by raising as many animals as possible within a given amount of space. The romanticized idea of animals contentedly grazing in green pastures on family farms has become a thing of the past for the vast majority of livestock. Modern farms commonly keep animals, in very close quarters and extremely confined. This practice makes it easier to maintain animals, thereby reducing the cost of labor. To keep animals in close confinement, farm managers have to use a variety of practices to maintain the health of their animals. Animal rights activists condemn many of these animal-management practices as cruel and inhumane.

Perhaps the most intensively managed farming involves the chicken, raised for both eggs and meat. Egg-laying chickens are kept in large barns in stacked wire cages containing seven to eight birds each, providing only about 60 square inches (387 sq. cm) of space per bird. These birds are so crowded they are unable to walk around or spread their wings. To prevent the chickens from pecking and harming each other, they are debeaked—a portion of their upper beaks is removed without anesthesia, or medicine to mask the pain.

Chickens raised for meat are kept in open pens and fed for rapid growth. By the age of six weeks, they have reached slaughter size

Animal rights activists say keeping animals in close confinement is cruel and inhumane. Here, a worker helps to clean a rat-infested chicken house where authorities found approximately one thousand dead chickens.

and have become crowded into a space of about 1 square foot (.09 sq. m) per bird. Because of their rapid growth, most suffer skeletal disorders that prevent them from walking properly.

Pigs raised in factory farms are also kept in extremely confined conditions. Sows, or female pigs, are kept for years in restrictive pregnancy and birthing crates just larger than their bodies, which prevent them from being able to turn around. Piglets raised for meat are moved into crowded pens after being neutered, having the ends of their canine teeth cut off, and having their tails removed to prevent injury to one another —all without anesthesia or painkillers. Shortly after birth many dairy calves raised for veal production are tethered in stalls, unable to move freely or sometimes even to turn around. They are given no opportunity to exercise and are fed a diet deficient in iron so that their meat will remain pale and tender when they are slaughtered at about three months of age.

THE VALUE OF ANIMALS

"All animals are equal but some animals are more equal than others." —George Orwell, noted mid-twentieth-century author.

George Orwell, *Animal Farm*. New York: Harcourt Brace, 1946, p. 109.

The practices employed in modern animal agriculture led authors Gaverick Matheny and Kai Chan to make this observation about the quality of life on the farm:

> These animals have retained instincts from their wild ancestors to explore their environments and develop complex social structures. But in intensive farms, many are confined in static environments, in unnatural group sizes, and exhibit signs of stress and frustration. If these animals' lives are worth living, we suspect they are barely so.[23]

While they admit some farming procedures could benefit from animal welfare improvements , industry experts cite many advantages to current practices. They insist that confinement farming allows them to better monitor the animals' health and

The Furor over Foie Gras

One of the gourmet food world's most prized delicacies is foie gras, the fattened liver of a duck or goose. For more than five thousand years, farmers have produced foie gras by force-feeding the birds through a tube placed down their throats during their last twelve to twenty-one days of life. The result is a greatly enlarged, richly flavored liver considered the ultimate ingredient in French cooking.

Campaigns by animal rights groups have drawn attention to what they say is the cruelty of the force-feeding practice. As a result, foie gras is facing increasing criticism by the general public and restaurant owners alike. In 2004 California passed a law banning force-feeding by 2012. Chicago has outlawed the sale of foie gras, and similar laws are being considered elsewhere. The issue gained widespread media attention when noted restaurant owner Wolfgang Puck vowed to stop serving foie gras at all his restaurants and catering facilities across the country.

While animal rights groups applaud these actions, some chefs see the move as slightly hypocritical. They believe that banning foie gras but continuing to serve other products produced by animals raised in ways that can also be inhumane makes little sense. Meanwhile foie gras producers seek alternative methods for fattening the livers of their birds without the need for force-feeding, in the hope they will be able to remain in business.

PETA members protest against foie gras. Many people are disturbed by the cruelty of the force-feeding practice that produces the richly flavored duck or goose liver.

nutrition, reduces the spread of disease with the use of well-ventilated and sanitary facilities, and provides the animals protection from predators and bad weather. In addition, they claim that these intensive facilities provide animals a less stressful setting for breeding and giving birth compared to animals living on free range. For example, farmers maintain that confining sows prevents them from crushing their offspring and reduces sow competition and fighting for food, as would happen if they were allowed to wander freely. "From an animal well-being standpoint, one must compare the benefits of producing cheaper pork, having a lowered mortality of piglets, and fewer injuries to the sows with the confinement housing that is required,"[24] states animal science professor Leland Shapiro.

Going to Slaughter

Not all food animals endure the harsh living conditions characterized by factory farming operations. Dairy cattle are usually given room to move more freely within barns and corrals. Beef

A cattle truck takes pigs to slaughter. The way animals are transported to slaughterhouses is a concern for animal rights groups.

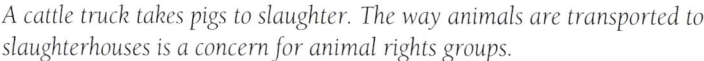

cattle spend time on both rangelands and more crowded feedlots. However, there are concerns about the welfare of cattle and other livestock during their transport to slaughterhouses as well as the methods for killing them and processing them into food.

Pigs, sheep, and cattle are transported from farms and feedlots to the slaughterhouse on tightly packed transport trucks or railcars. During transport, the animals may be subjected to temperature extremes and lack food and water, often for more than twenty-four hours. Animal rights groups claim that many animals are injured or die during transport due to trampling, freezing, or dehydration.

Once at the slaughterhouse, animals are supposed to be killed according to the guidelines outlined in the Humane Slaughter Act, a law enacted in 1958 to minimize the suffering of animals killed for food. The law requires cattle, hogs, sheep, and horses to be made unconscious by a blow to the head with a stun gun or electric shock prior to slaughter so that they are not able to feel pain. However, animal rights organizations claim—and the farming industry acknowledges—that proper stunning does not always take place. In those cases, animals that are still conscious may continue down the line that processes carcasses.

Violation records, videotapes, and interviews with slaughterhouse workers support these claims. "They blink. They make noises. The head moves, the eyes are wide and looking around,"[25] says one slaughterhouse worker who regularly sees animals being processed while they are still conscious. Veterinarian Lester Friedlander, a former government inspector at a hamburger plant, also supports these claims. "In plants all over the United States, this happens on a daily basis," he says. "I've seen it happen. And I've talked to other veterinarians. They feel it's out of control."[26]

One reason slaughterhouses give for why they violate the Humane Slaughter Act is the rate at which animals are processed. In some factories, over three hundred animals go down the production line each hour. At these large factories cattle are stunned and hoisted onto an overhead chain within twelve seconds of entering the killing chamber. This rate provides workers little time to accurately stun the animals, forcing them to send them down the line even if they are still conscious.

Religious Slaughter: Culture or Cruelty?

The Humane Slaughter Act contains provisions that allow the slaughter of animals using special practices required for religious purposes. Both Jewish kosher slaughter and Muslim halal slaughter prohibit the use of stunning prior to killing the animals. Both of these practices require the animal's throat to be cut, causing the animal to bleed to death. Until recently this type of slaughter was performed on animals, including large cattle, that were hoisted fully conscious by their back legs before being killed. Due to welfare concerns, most animals are now killed while in a standing position in a special restraint device that allows the butcher to make a rapid cut.

Despite this advance, some people condemn this method of slaughter. They claim that the animal may take one to two minutes to bleed to death, during which time they experience pain and fear. They believe that animal welfare should take priority when expressing religious freedom causes unnecessary suffering. Others counter that the animals do not suffer and believe that freedom to practice religion in their own way is much more important than the welfare of an animal. The United Kingdom proposed a ban on religious slaughter that was defeated in 2004. This controversial issue will likely be an ongoing source of debate.

Animal science experts who work in the meat industry continue to seek ways to improve the slaughtering process in an effort to enhance animal welfare. Dr. Temple Grandin, an animal sciences professor at Colorado State University, advises slaughterhouses on ways to design facilities and handle animals that would minimize fear and ensure animals are killed humanely. She stresses that plants could easily make small changes that would take animals' natural instincts into account. For example, workers could move more quietly, and the slaughterhouses could eliminate shadows that tend to spook animals. These actions would result in animals that move more calmly and thus allow for much more accurate stunning.

Grandin also points out that humane slaughter is much more likely when meat buyers monitor the factories. Some fast-food chains, such as McDonald's and Wendy's, conduct audits of factories and will not buy meat from facilities where abuses are recorded. Grandin says, "In the U.S., some really atrocious abuses occurred in pork and beef plants that were not audited by a restaurant or supermarket. . . . Audits by restaurant companies have brought about big improvements in the handling and stunning of cattle and pigs. One of the most effective ways to improve animal welfare in slaughter plants is for large corporations to use their buying power to improve conditions."[27]

Improving Conditions for Meat Animals

Improvements are gradually coming to some areas of food-animal production. McDonald's, Wendy's, and Burger King have announced that they will give preference to companies that improve animal welfare standards when buying meat and eggs for their restaurants. These companies have goals that include buying eggs from facilities that allow chickens more freedom of

Dorothy Egg Farms in Winthrop, Maine, has a cage-free house for chickens. Many companies now give preference to companies that take animal welfare standards into account when producing their products.

movement, known as "cage-free eggs." They also plan to purchase a greater percentage of pork each year from farms that do not keep sows in highly restrictive pens.

There are also signs of fading use of confinement crates for sows and veal calves, long considered among the most brutal farming practices. The European Union has already outlawed the use of sow and veal crates by the year 2013. Arizona, Florida, and Oregon have passed laws banning the practice, and other states are looking at similar legislation. Increasing pressure from both animal rights organizations and consumers have also led to some industry leaders voluntarily pledging to end the use of confinement pens. Strauss Veal, the largest veal producer in the United States, has abandoned the use of veal crates completely and instead raises its calves in group pens or with their mothers on pasture. "Animal rights are important," company owner Randy Strauss says. "We want to be the company to revolutionize the veal industry."[28]

Better Treatment Makes a Better Product

"If we feed the animals better, treat them better, we will have a better product and a healthier product." —Wolfgang Puck, celebrity chef and restaurant owner.

Quoted in Marian Burros, "Veal to Love, Without the Guilt," *New York Times*, April 18, 2007, p. F1.

In early 2007 the world's largest pork producer, Smithfield Foods, announced it would phase out the use of confinement pens for sows in its 187 U.S. farms over the next ten years. Company executives deny that this move was a result of pressure from animal rights activists or the recent passage of laws banning crates. Instead, they say, they are responding to their customers' concerns. "We are trying to be proactive and respond to what we think the customers want,"[29] explains Dennis Treacy, a Smithfield vice president. Wayne Pacelle, president of the Humane Society of the United States, applauds this precedent-setting decision. "This is perhaps the most important moment in animal

Slaughter of Horses

Although few people in the United States would consider eating meat from horses, in some countries such as France, Belgium, Italy, and Japan, horsemeat is considered a delicacy. Few people realize that until recently, the United States slaughtered tens of thousands of horses each year in order to export their meat to feed foreign consumers. These horses came from all segments of the horse industry, including family pets, horses sold at auction, retired racehorses, and horses stolen to be sold for meat. Although the last American horse slaughterhouses have been closed after a ban on the production of meat for human consumption, horses are still being trucked to processing facilities in Mexico and Canada.

This practice greatly concerns animal rights advocates and horse lovers across the United States. Horses are usually transported to slaughter long distances in trucks designed for cattle. Horses cannot lift their heads in these trucks and often slip and fall, becoming injured during transport. Conditions in Mexican slaughterhouses have been documented to be inhumane, causing severe suffering to horses killed there. To prevent such cruelty, horse advocates are supporting the passage of a new law to prohibit the shipment of horses for slaughter.

welfare in the agribusiness sector in 50 years,"[30] he says. "They are the market leader, and this decision changes the dynamic of the industry. It's going to be very hard for other companies to not follow Smithfield."[31]

Many animal rights groups are campaigning for additional changes to reduce the suffering of farm animals. Currently the billions of chickens and turkeys processed for food annually are exempt from the provisions of the Humane Slaughter Act. These birds are suspended alive by their legs on an overhead conveyor system and stunned by an electric current. Incomplete stunning may result in their being slaughtered while they are still able to feel pain. Animal rights groups, as well as large poultry buyers such as McDonald's and Wendy's, advocate a more humane method of killing chickens. This method, called "controlled atmospheric stunning," exposes the poultry to a gas that allows them to calmly fall unconscious in their transport cages prior to slaughter. This method is already in use in Europe.

Vegetarianism

Even if laws are strengthened and practices altered to promote better welfare for farm animals, animal rights supporters are unlikely to support arguments that livestock farming can ever be humane. Most argue against any use of animals for human benefit, including food, and urge people to adopt a vegetarian lifestyle. Although the nutritional benefits of eating meat and dairy products are well established, proponents of a vegetarian diet point out that humans do not need to eat meat in order to be healthy. A well-managed, plant-based diet can provide all the nutrients essential for life. In fact, much evidence suggests that

Animal rights activists promote a vegetarian diet. Most vegetarians argue that the use of animals for human benefit, including food, is wrong.

plant-based diets are healthier than meat-based diets, which are often linked to obesity, heart disease, and cancer.

Many meat eaters acknowledge the health benefits of being a vegetarian and understand the consequences of eating meat on farm animal welfare. However, some people hesitate to adopt a vegetarian diet because they believe it is inconvenient or costs more than a meat-eating diet. In addition, many people simply enjoy meat too much to give it up. According to Francione, this attitude is morally unacceptable:

> Regrettably for those who like to eat meat, this is no argument, and a taste for meat in no way justifies the violation of a moral principle. Our conduct merely demonstrates that despite what we say about the moral significance of animal interests, we are willing to ignore those interests whenever we benefit from doing so—even when the benefit is nothing more than our pleasure or convenience.[32]

A Vegetarian World

"I believe a vegetarian world would be a more compassionate world." —Mark Bekoff, professor and author of many books on animal behavior and emotions.

Mark Bekoff, *The Emotional Lives of Animals*. Novato, CA: New World Library, 2007, p. 151.

The recent shift in attitude of both meat producers and consumers may indicate a growing concern for improving food-animal welfare. Ron Paul, president of a company that advises meat producers, believes, "There is a growing realization that the humane movement is a long-term movement. It's not going to go away."[33]

Author Ron Scully is an active campaigner for reforming the food-animal industry and wants to hold producers to a higher standard. "We cannot just take from these creatures, we must give them something in return," he says. "We owe them a merciful death, and we owe them a merciful life."[34]

Animal Experimentation

One of the most hotly debated ways in which humans use animals is as research subjects for scientific experiments. Nearly 22 million animals are used for research annually in the United States. Most research animals are rodents, such as rats and mice, and are specifically bred for this use. Dogs and cats account for 1 to 1.5 percent of research animals. Primates—monkeys and apes—make up less than 0.5 percent. Other animals used for research include rabbits, pigs, cattle, and sharks.

Many people believe that these research animals play a vital role in advancing human medicine and safety. Others, however, consider animal experimentation to be both cruel and unnecessary. Animal rights organizations have mounted vocal campaigns against animal research that have led to a decline in the use of animal testing by 50 percent since the 1970s. Despite this decline, many scientists, doctors, and members of the general public still strongly support animal research because of the benefits it provides to people.

Using Animals to Study Biology and Behavior

Virtually everyone living today has benefited from the use of live animals in scientific study. Countless medicines, vaccines, surgical procedures, diagnostic tests, and other medical treatments were either discovered or tested through experiments with animals. Since animals became commonly used in research in the early 1900s, advances in medicine have helped increased human life span by 60 percent, from an average of forty-seven years to seventy-five years today. Two-thirds of the Nobel prizes awarded in medicine or physiology in the twentieth century were given to scientists who used animal subjects in their research. Some of the most notable advances resulting from animal research include vaccines for infectious diseases such as polio and rabies, antibiotics such as penicillin, and medical procedures such as open-heart surgery and X-rays.

Animals are used in research for several purposes. One is to research behavior. By studying what factors influence the way creatures behave, researchers have made many significant advances in the treatment of conditions such as drug and alcohol addiction and mental illness. Behavioral studies on cats resulted in discoveries that led to the development of treatments for strokes and brain damage. Behavioral research is also helping scientists better understand the connection between the body and mind, which can influence diseases such as those relating to stress.

THE BUNNY OR THE CHILD?

"Which of us, told that our son or daughter has been diagnosed with cancer, would say 'save the bunny rabbit, [damn] the child?'" —Trevor Philips, a columnist writing in the *Independent*, a United Kingdom newspaper.

Trevor Philips, "Human Self-Interest Will Ensure That Animal Experimentation Continues," quoted in David M. Haugen, ed., *Animal Experimentation*. San Diego: Greenhaven, 2000, p. 39.

Another reason why scientists use animals in research is to better understand how living bodies function and how they respond to diseases and medical treatments and procedures. Animals are used as models for humans in these studies because they have complex body systems that behave in much the same way human bodies do. In order for their studies to be as useful as possible, researchers seek out the best animal model for each experiment. Sometimes animals are selected for study because they suffer from the same diseases as humans. For example, rabbits are studied for the eye disease glaucoma, mice are studied for epilepsy, and cats are studied for deafness.

Other animals are selected for studies based on their size. Dogs and pigs have organs similar in size to those of humans. As

This dairy cow, a cross between a Jersey and an Indian red sindhi, is being studied to develop a heat-resistant breed for use in the southern United States.

a result, they are commonly used for research on joint replacements, heart disease, organ transplants, and surgical techniques. Despite their small size, rodents are some of the most commonly used animals in research. Because rats have short life spans of two to three years, researchers conducting studies on aging or the progression of disease can gain results relatively quickly.

Another advantage to using rodents in research is that they can be used in large numbers. Scientists can select individuals that share certain characteristics, such as age and size, so they can determine if their findings might apply to large populations. In addition, their rapid rate of reproduction makes them useful for studies on genetics and other studies that require observation over many generations. Rodents can also be selectively bred to be prone to certain diseases, such as cancer, that will allow researchers to study ways to treat or prevent those conditions.

Opposition to Animals in Medical Research

Despite the growing movement to limit animal research, supporters of animal rights insist that the use of animals for scientific study should end completely. They cite instances of abuse and neglect that they say are the result of cruel and careless researchers. They also claim that animals used in research

The LD-50 Test

One of the most controversial tests performed on animals is known as the Lethal Dose 50 (LD-50) test, used to measure the toxicity of drugs or other chemicals. This test is used to determine what amount of a substance will kill 50 percent of the test population within a certain period of time. In this test, animals are given a dose of a substance by force-feeding, through injection, or by application to the skin and observed for signs of toxicity. Researchers use the results of this test to determine what dosage of the chemical would be harmful to humans.

Because large numbers of animals, sometimes as many as one hundred, die painfully as a result of a single test, the LD-50 test has been widely criticized for being cruel. In addition, many people question the accuracy of the test. Results vary widely among species and are affected by the age and gender of test subjects, the dosing technique, and conditions in the lab. These variations lead many to doubt the test's ability to predict a human's reaction to the substance. Due to these concerns, the LD-50 test has been banned in the United Kingdom, and its use is on the decline elsewhere. Although a non-animal alternative to the LD-50 test has not yet been found, another test called the Fixed Dose Procedure is frequently used instead. This test uses a smaller number of animals to find a dose that causes signs of toxicity, but not death. Scientists use the results to calculate the dosage that would be lethal.

experience suffering as a result of confinement to cages and pain from experiments. Activists are especially opposed to experiments involving surgery on living animals, a practice known as vivisection.

Opponents of animal experimentation argue that many diseases afflicting people such as cancer, heart disease, and diabetes are strongly linked to lifestyle choices such as diet and exercise. Therefore, they insist, scientists should put a greater focus on the prevention of these diseases instead of their treatment. They also believe that using animals in research has limited value for improving human health. Advances in human life span and the decline of killer disease outbreaks are more a result of improved sanitation and better diet than treatments developed through animal studies, they argue.

The Evil

"When you start with a necessary evil, and then over time the necessity passes away, what's left?" —Matthew Scully, a former speechwriter for President George W. Bush, author, and supporter of animal rights.

Matthew Scully, *Dominion*. New York: St. Martin's, 2002, p. 386.

Testing Drug and Product Safety

Another reason animals are used in research is to determine if products are safe for use by humans. These products include medicines, chemicals, and items used around the home. When new products are developed, scientists often conduct toxicity tests on animals to determine what effects the products will have on the animals and how the products will react in the animals' bodies. Animals are exposed to the products through a variety of methods. One way is by feeding the product to the animal. If the product is a new drug, for example, this testing allows researchers to determine if the drug is safe and at what dosage levels, or amount, it is most effective. If the results of testing a product on an animal show that its use may be harmful, manufacturers improve the product or determine requirements for using it safely.

Not all toxicity tests require animals to ingest products. In some tests, animals may have to inhale a chemical, or researchers may apply a product to an animal's eyes or skin to see if the product is harmful. While many of the products tested on animals play an important role in human health or are vital to society, sometimes tests involve nonessential products, such as cosmetics.

One of the most controversial tests used for this purpose is the Draize test, named after a scientist working for the U.S. Food and Drug Administration in the 1940s. The Draize test involves putting chemicals in the eyes of rabbits to determine whether or not a product will irritate or harm the eyes. Rabbits

A rabbit undergoes an experiment to see what effect laser light has on its eye. Many animals are used in research to determine product safety.

in the test are restrained so that they cannot move their heads. The substance being tested is applied to the rabbits' eyes, and then researchers observe the effects, designating a score corresponding to the amount of irritation. This test was once commonly used to test products such as makeup and shampoo.

Animal rights groups vocally criticized such research as cruel, which led to public outcry against the test. As a result, since the 1980s the number of rabbits used for testing in the cosmetics industry has been reduced by 87 percent, and many cosmetic companies have abandoned the practice of testing their products on animals completely. Instead these companies use ingredients already proven safe or use human volunteers in their product testing. These companies often use the fact that they do not test on animals as a marketing tool. Their products often bear labels identifying them as "cruelty free" or "not tested on animals."

Criticism of Using Animals as Human Models

Animal rights supporters criticize the use of animals to test drugs or product safety. They say animals are poor models for the development of medical treatments for humans, citing cases in which animals respond to diseases and medicines differently than humans do. For example, research showed penicillin to be deadly to hamsters and guinea pigs. In contrast, other tests show that some chemicals dangerous to people have little impact on animal health. When exposed to cigarette smoke, dogs and monkeys failed to develop lung cancer. Animal research opponents claim that results such as these have hindered human health by delaying the release of treatments that benefit people or held up health warnings about dangerous products. Veterinarian Jean Greek and her husband, Ray Greek, a doctor, are outspoken critics of the usefulness of using animals in medical research. They have analyzed the role of animals in medical advancements and believe that applying results from animal studies to humans is difficult and even dangerous.

> We were finding, through scientific research, that extrapolating data from animals to humans is either misleading, unnecessary, dangerous, or all three. . . . Since

Genetic Engineering

One of the newest and most rapidly advancing areas of animal research is the field of biotechnology, sometimes called genetic engineering. Biotechnologists make small changes to the genetic code of an animal, which allows them to create animals that they can then use to research genetic diseases that affect humans, including cancer, diabetes, and obesity. By creating animal models with the genes for these diseases, researchers can better understand how genes influence disease, develop treatments for disease, and limit the number of research animals required for studies.

In addition to providing models for human diseases, genetic engineering also enables researchers to put copies of human genes into animals so that the animals produce compounds used in human medicine. For example, a sheep's genes could be altered so that it produces a protein used for treating patients with a bleeding disorder. This sheep could then be cloned, creating exact copies of the genetically engineered animal able to produce the human protein. These genetically identical animals would serve as a pharmaceutical "factory," providing a source of the protein for treating patients. Some researchers are also working to develop genetically engineered animals that will be able to serve as organ donors for people.

Opponents of biotechnology fear that there may be negative consequences of altering genes that are not yet apparent. The behavior of these genes over the long term is not yet known, and some altered animals have demonstrated shortened life spans and greater susceptibility to disease. Critics also raise ethical objections to the use of animals as profit-making medical factories and fear the development of large-scale farms for genetically altered animals.

---

we are all putting our lives and the lives of our loved ones in the hands of supposedly rigorous science, is not a model that requires so much fudging grossly inadequate —especially since humans themselves provide the perfect model?[35]

Although humans are the perfect model for testing the effects of drugs and other medical treatments, safety concerns mean that people are used only during the final stages of testing. After conducting rigorous tests on animals in the lab, researchers perform tests on human patients during clinical trials. These trials determine the proper amounts and best ways to administer the drug or treatment. Often drugs never advance beyond these trials, because they are not effective enough or cause undesirable side effects. Using people to test potentially dangerous chemicals or drugs suspected of causing birth defects without examining the effects on animals beforehand could cause irreversible damage to the human subjects.

Animal Experiments in Education

In addition to their role as subjects for developing medical treatments or testing products, animals are also commonly used for educational purposes. Many animals, including invertebrates, frogs, cats, and pigs, are frequently used as dissection subjects to teach biology to students in classrooms from elementary school to college. Although these animals are already dead when they reach the classroom, they were killed specifically for the lesson. Living animals are also frequently used for educational training purposes, such as to provide doctors and veterinarians with opportunities to practice surgery and other procedures.

The role of animals in education is becoming increasingly controversial. Some animal rights activists insist that the use of animals as substitutes for humans for training doctors has limited value because of their differences in anatomy. Instead they support the use of human cadavers. Some people also consider the use of animals for dissection in the classroom as outdated and unnecessary. To address these concerns, alternatives such as plastic models and computer programs that simulate dissection are now available. And where participation in classroom dissections was once required, in many cases students morally opposed to animal experimentation may now choose not to participate in the lesson or select an alternative instead.

The Use of Primates in Research

The most frequently criticized form of animal research is the use of nonhuman primates—monkeys and apes such as chimpanzees—as test subjects. Because primates are so similar to people, they serve as models for researchers to study many human diseases such as AIDS, hepatitis, osteoporosis, heart disease,

A Retirement Home for Chimps

In 2000, President Bill Clinton signed the CHIMP (Chimpanzee Health Improvement, Maintenance, and Protection) Act into law. This law acknowledged that the United States has a moral responsibility to provide lifetime care for chimpanzees used in medical research conducted or supported by the federal government. The CHIMP Act provides federal funding for the creation of sanctuaries for housing chimps no longer needed for research purposes.

The first sanctuary established as a result of the CHIMP Act is Louisiana's Chimp Haven. Since 2005, over one hundred chimps once used in research by the National Institutes of Health have found a new life in retirement at this nonprofit sanctuary supported by both federal funds and private donations. Chimp Haven's setting on 200 acres (81ha) in the lush and humid countryside provides a more natural life for the chimps, some of which had been taken from the wild before living for decades in a laboratory.

After they acclimate to their new home, chimps at Chimp Haven are kept in natural social groupings and given access to large outdoor play yards, indoor bedrooms, and items that allow them to stay both mentally and physically active. Because of their lack of experience in a natural setting, many of the chimps are hesitant to climb trees or explore the surrounding meadows. To encourage this behavior, caregivers place treats in trees and scatter food for the chimps to discover. Chimp Haven plans to expand in the future, eventually providing a home for two hundred chimpanzees.

Lolita, a chimpanzee, is now a resident at Chimp Haven in Keithville, Louisiana, after spending years in a biomedical research lab.

Parkinson's disease, and drug addiction. The similarities between primates and humans also make primates good subjects for studying biological processes such as reproduction and aging. In addition, their intelligence and social systems make primates ideal candidates for the study of language, learning, memory, and other skills requiring complex thinking or social interaction.

The same qualities that make primates such good models for humans, however, also suggest that they experience suffering in much the same way that humans do. Animal rights activists

A baby chimpanzee is used in AIDS research. Primates are often used by researchers to study human diseases because of their similarities to humans.

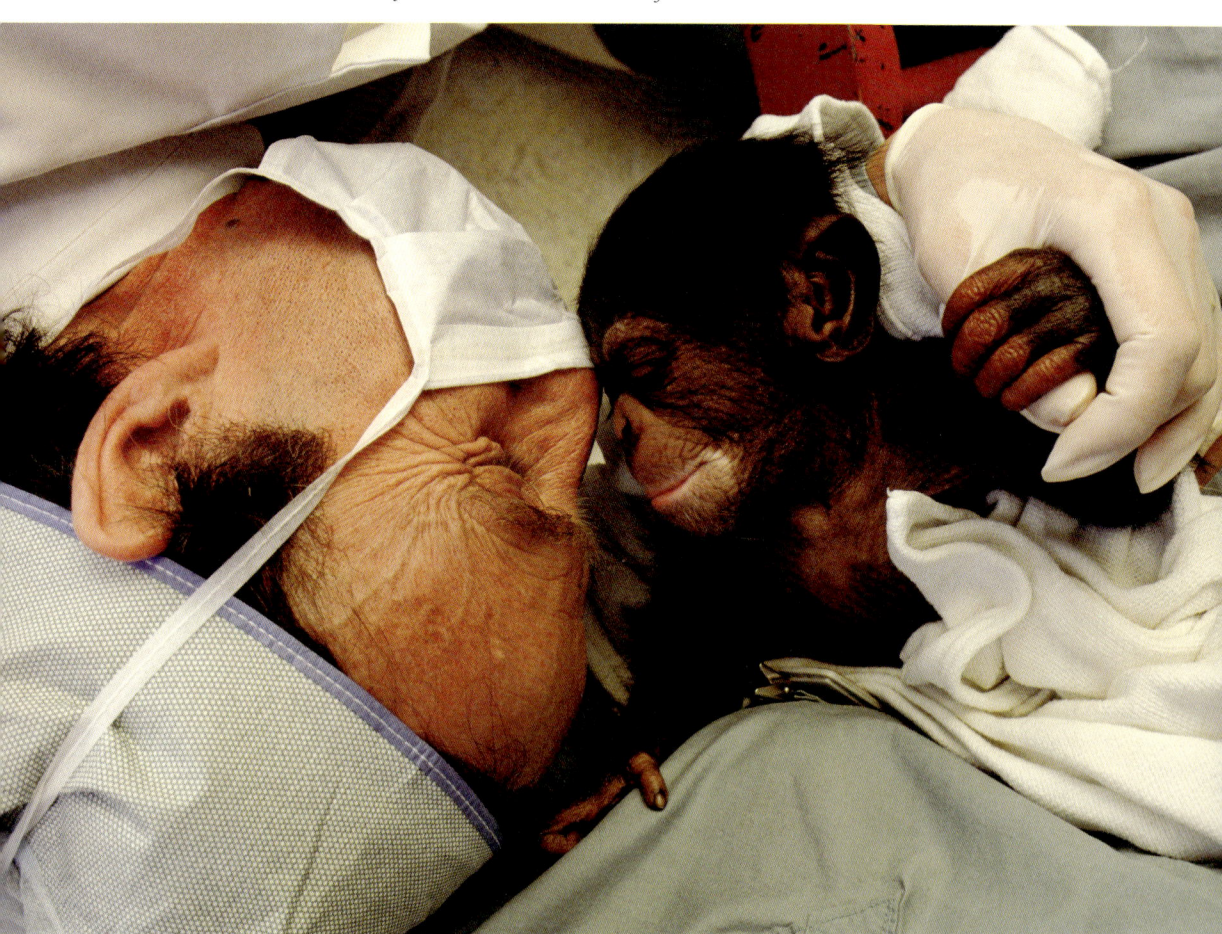

insist that using primates for research subjects them to extreme suffering due to pain and isolation in small cages. Many of the approximately fifty thousand primates used in research in the United States are housed in eight national primate research centers funded by the federal government for research to benefit human health. Some of the primates in these centers are maintained in large enclosures providing natural social groupings, and others are kept as individuals or small groups in more confining cages.

Some primate research is relatively harmless to the animals—researchers simply observe their behavior without causing any physical injury. Other research is more invasive, however, and involves surgery, restraint, blood draws, and other procedures that can cause pain and anxiety. Some primates are kept in labs and used for many different studies over the course of several years or even decades. Other studies require that the animals be euthanized at the end of the test so that their organs and tissues can be examined after death.

Animal rights activists strongly oppose the use of primates in such research. Jane Goodall, a pioneer in the study of wild chimpanzees, cried upon seeing a caged chimp in a visit to a research lab. After viewing the cramped and sterile living conditions of animals she knew firsthand to be intelligent and active creatures, Goodall became an outspoken critic of the use of chimps for research purposes. "Humans are a species capable of compassion, and we should develop a heightened moral responsibility for beings who are so like ourselves,"[36] she said.

Animal Research Standards

Most researchers have great concern for the welfare of their subjects and go to great lengths to provide the most humane care possible. The use of animals in medical research is regulated by the provisions of the Animal Welfare Act (AWA), a law passed in 1966 to provide minimum standards of care and treatment for certain laboratory animals, including dogs, cats, and primates. The AWA dictates the minimum allowable cage space, as well as standards for feeding, exercise, and social groupings of animals. Research facilities are also required to have an Institutional

Facts About the Animal Welfare Act

- Passed by Congress in 1966 and strengthened through amendments in 1970, 1976, 1985, and 1990.

- Includes: animals bred for commercial sale, used in research, transported commercially, or exhibited to the public.

- Does not include: farm animals used for food, fiber, or other agricultural purposes and coldblooded animals (such as snakes and alligators).

- Retail pet shops are not covered under the Act unless the shop sells exotic or zoo animals, or sells animals to regulated businesses.

- Animal shelters and pounds are regulated if they sell dogs or cats to dealers.

- Animal dealers must hold the animals that they acquire for 5–10 days to verify origin and allow pet owners an opportunity to locate a missing pet.

- Prohibits staged animal-fighting ventures.

- All individuals or businesses that deal with animals under the Act must be licensed or registered with the USDA Animal and Plant Health Inspection Service.

- Performs regular inspections, conducts reviews, and investigates alleged violations. Also will perform inspections in response to public input about conditions at regulated facilities or unlicensed facilities that should be licensed.

Taken from: United States Department of Agriculture, Animal and Plant Health Inspection Service. Available online at: www.aphis.usda.gov/publications/animal_welfare/content/printable_version/fs_awawact.pdf.

Animal Care and Use Committee (IACUC) to oversee research activities. The IACUC reviews and monitors the studies to ensure that the use of animals is both necessary and humane.

Despite its significant role in addressing the humane treatment of laboratory animals, the AWA does not go nearly far enough, according to critics of animal testing. The AWA regulations do not cover the care and use of birds, farm animals, and rodents, which represent about 80 percent of all animals used in research. Due to poor funding, there are limited numbers of inspectors available to monitor labs with the frequency necessary to be sure they comply with the law. IACUCs, too, are criticized for sometimes not setting strict enough standards for approving research proposals. Because many studies bring significant grant funding to the research facility, IACUCs may approve proposals that have little scientific merit.

WOULD YOU DO IT TO YOUR DOG?

"When it comes to the sometimes unconscious double standard that people frequently have in the treatment of animals, I find the question 'Would you do it to your dog?' to be a great leveler. If you wouldn't do something to your dog, why would you do it to any other being?" —Mark Bekoff, professor and author of many books on animal behavior and emotions.

Mark Bekoff, *The Emotional Lives of Animals*. Novato, CA: New World Library, 2007, p. 22.

Although they do not agree with claims that animals in labs are mistreated and suffer, researchers do share some of the concerns of those who oppose animal testing. To demonstrate that the scientific community has genuine concern for the treatment of their laboratory animals, they follow a set of guiding principles known as the Three Rs (reduce, refine, and replace). The Three Rs recognize that the use of animals in research to benefit humans is necessary but can be done in a way that is both scientifically and ethically valid.

Reduce means to limit the number of animals required for an experiment. Selecting the number of animals for a study is a

Scientist John McArdle, pictured here in 2001, believes that animals shouldn't suffer unnecessarily and promotes alternatives to animal experimentation.

precise science; use too few and the results will not be statistically valid, use more than necessary and the lives of animals will be wasted needlessly.

Refine means to design experiments in ways to minimize the amount of suffering for the animals involved. If the research is painful, animals must be given anesthesia or painkillers. If the study involves a painful or fatal disease, animals may be euthanized when symptoms begin instead of waiting for the animal to suffer a long and painful death. Refinement also includes improving the quality of everyday life for lab animals by providing nesting materials, toys, and interesting food items.

Replace means that, whenever possible, experiments should be conducted without using animals at all. However, while there have been some successes in finding new ways to conduct experiments that eliminate the need for animals, progress in this area is slow.

Alternatives to the Use of Animals

The ethics of using animals in research is a driving force behind the search for alternatives, but it is not the only one. Animal research is time consuming, expensive, and not always accurate, so research facilities are eager to find other ways to develop new drugs or test the toxicity of chemicals. One advancement is the ability of researchers to grow both animal and human cell and tissue cultures in the laboratory. These living cultures are used to study the effects of drugs in treating cancer, AIDS, diabetes, and other diseases.

> ### VITAL TO MEDICINE
>
> "Animals will continue to be as vital as the scientists who study them in the battle to eliminate pain, suffering and disease from our lives. That is the reality of medical progress." —Heloisa Sabin, honorary director of Americans for Medical Progress, a group supporting the use of animals in research.
>
> Heloisa Sabin, "Animal Research Saves Human Lives," quoted in David M. Haugen, ed., *Animal Experimentation*. San Diego: Greenhaven, 2000, p. 12.

Powerful computer programs are now available to model disease processes in humans, replacing animal tests for certain studies. Computerized databases also maintain information so that tests are not repeated needlessly. In addition, computers are able to identify patterns or trends in diseases that may allow researchers to eliminate more basic studies. Many new technologies, such as magnetic resonance imaging, allow researchers to see inside the bodies of people and animals without causing harm.

While researchers embrace advances that limit the need for animal testing, most believe that alternatives will never replace the use of animals entirely. So far, at least, these alternatives are unable to completely duplicate the complex biology of living animals. In its statement on the use of animals in research, the American Medical Association explains:

> No other method of study can exactly reproduce the characteristics and qualities of a living intact biological system

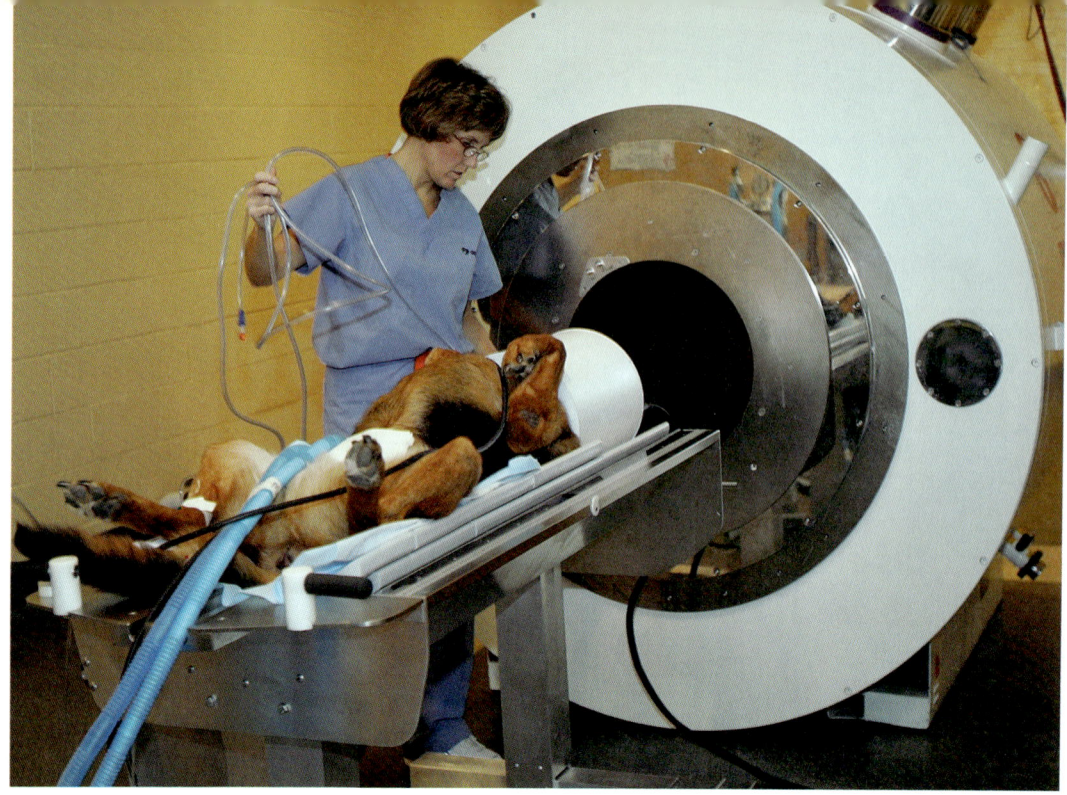

Magnetic resonance imaging (MRI) machines allow researchers to see inside the bodies of people and animals without causing harm. Here, a technician prepares a dog for an MRI exam.

or organism. Therefore, in order to understand how such a system or organism functions in a particular set of circumstances or how it will react to a given stimulus, it becomes necessary at some point to conduct an experiment or test to find out. There simply is no alternative to this approach and therefore no alternative to using animals for most types of health related research.[37]

Although both researchers and animal rights groups would like to see an end to animal research, it appears likely that they will remain opponents for many years to come.

Animals in Sport and Entertainment

Animals have played a significant role in sports and entertainment throughout history, and some of these practices are deeply rooted in human culture. Animals are used for human amusement in a wide variety of ways. Some celebrate the animals' beauty, strength, and speed. In contrast, animals are also harmed or killed to entertain people.

Supporters of animal rights are concerned about many of the ways in which animals are used in sports and entertainment. They feel that forcing animals to compete in sports for human benefit is cruel. They claim that these sports promote large-scale suffering of animals as a result of overbreeding, mistreatment, poor veterinary care, and disposal of unwanted animals. Most animal rights activists support ending all uses of animals in sports and entertainment.

People who support the use of animals in sports claim that the animals are simply doing what comes naturally to them, such as running or fighting. They also argue that many uses of animals in sports and entertainment provide cultural benefits and are part of long-standing human traditions.

Blood Sports

Some of the earliest uses of animals in entertainment took place in the time of the ancient Romans. Emperors commonly arranged for wild animals to be captured in Africa and brought to amphitheaters for elaborate shows featuring animal fights and simulated hunts. Before thousands of cheering spectators, lions, leopards, elephants, crocodiles, giraffes, hippos, and rhinoceroses would fight one another or be killed by Roman gladiators. On special occasions honoring an emperor's inauguration or achievements in battle, thousands of wild animals were killed over several weeks of festivities. These lavish displays of animals from exotic locations were used to signify the wealth and power of the reigning leader.

These often brutal acts of entertainment involving animals were not just limited to ancient times. As recently as the 1800s, the practices of "bearbaiting" and "bullbaiting" were still popular in England. These events featured a bear or bull chained to a post in the center of a public arena. Trained dogs would attack the animal, eventually killing it. Often several of the at-

The Role of Zoos

Each year over 143 million people in North America visit zoos and aquariums accredited by the Association of Zoos and Aquariums. These zoo visits provide opportunities for people to see and learn about wildlife from all over the world through exhibits, classes, and other presentations. Zoos are also active in conservation efforts for many endangered animals. Each year they spend millions of dollars to study and preserve hundreds of species both in captivity and in their wild habitats.

Many animal rights organizations insist, however, that zoos are little more than collections of caged animals and that they do little to educate the public on wildlife-conservation issues. Activists claim that most people visit zoos for entertainment, not education. They insist that wildlife education can be better achieved through film documentaries instead of keeping animals in captivity. They also claim that most zoo exhibits are unable to provide environments that encourage animals to behave naturally. As a result, they believe that animals suffer both mentally and physically from being deprived of their freedom.

Zoo supporters counter that zoos provide opportunities for families to connect with animals on a personal basis, fostering feelings of amazement and appreciation of the natural world. These feelings lead people to consider their role in protecting the environment. Many zoos are now studying the ways that people learn during their visits. Their discoveries will help zoos design exhibits and programs that are even more valuable for developing environmental awareness and encouraging visitors to participate in conservation efforts.

tacking dogs were killed in the process. Due to rising public outcry against such events, in 1835 the Cruelty to Animals Act was passed that banned the practice. While bearbaiting no longer takes place, other sports featuring animals fighting or being killed continue. Although outlawed in some regions, these "blood sports" such as dogfighting, bullfighting, and cockfighting still occur both in public and in private in many places around the world.

A Dark Place

"There is a dark place in the human soul that is expressed in a small number of people in violence toward animals." —Wayne Pacelle, president, Humane Society of the United States.

Quoted in Peter Whoriskey, "Cockfighting on the Web Enters Legal Arena," *Washington Post*, July 22, 2007, p. A3.

Bullfighting

One of the most controversial sports involving the killing of animals is bullfighting. Although its history is uncertain, the sport may have descended from earlier contests between people and animals in ancient Rome. Today's bullfighting is firmly rooted in Spain, where it has been practiced for more than one thousand years. It is also popular in France, Portugal, Mexico, and some other Latin American countries.

As a bullfight begins, men on horseback spear a bull in the neck and shoulders. Next, other men move in on foot to thrust barbed sticks into the bull's back to further enrage it. As blood flows from its wounds, the bull charges the matador who encourages it to attack by waving his cape. The matador is applauded for close brushes with the bull's lethal horns as he smoothly dodges the angry animal running by. Finally, as the bull weakens, the matador stabs it between the shoulder blades with his sword to make the kill. Depending on the quality of the matador's performance, the judge may grant him the privilege of slicing off the bull's ears and tail as tokens symbolizing his courage.

Supporters of bullfighting praise the matadors' technique and bravery, comparing them to gifted artists. Isabel Carpio, secretary-general of the Union of Fighting Bull Breeders views the contest as beautiful and believes that a top matador "is like a sculptor who is molding, not clay, but the animal."[38] Many also cite bullfighting's strong historic connection to a region's culture. "It is a cultural component that comes from times that we no longer even remember," says a young Spanish woman attending a bullfight. "It is something that is ours, something intrinsic. It is a world that once you enter, you like it more and more, and you want to be more a part of it."[39]

Other advocates of bullfighting include the king of Spain and other top politicians and celebrities in that country, many of

Bullfighting critics point out that, in addition to the killing of the bull, many horses also die in the ring after being gored by enraged bulls.

whom share the viewpoint of the supporters of the sport. "There is something incredibly powerful about a man trying to stand as still as possible and to dominate and control a wild animal that's trying to kill him, and at the same moment creates incredibly subtle, beautiful, delicate artistic images,"[40] explains one fan. "Good bulls are noble: they humiliate the bullfighter and do not fear him," says one matador. "When I kill a bull, I don't think about it. It is just another movement in a bullfight, and this movement is to kill."[41]

In contrast to its supporters, many people view bullfighting as an outdated sport that promotes the torture and suffering of animals. Critics claim that the time in the ring is extremely stressful and painful for the bull. Estimates vary, but at least twelve thousand bulls are killed in Spain alone each year during bullfights. Many horses also die in the ring after being gored by enraged bulls. Miguel Moutinho, the leader of a Portuguese animal welfare group, expresses scorn toward matadors. "Bullfighters like to say they are artists but [the bullfighter] is a murderer and bullfighting is an immoral spectacle,"[42] he says.

Both opinion polls and bullring attendance show that support for bullfighting is declining, even in Spain. Animal rights groups regularly stage protests outside bullfighting arenas and are pressuring the government to ban the practice. Spain already has strict laws against animal cruelty, but those laws make exceptions for bullfighting. "Bullfighting is terrible savagery and should be consigned to history,"[43] says one activist.

Fighting Birds

Another common blood sport held in many parts of the world is cockfighting. Cockfighting takes advantage of a rooster's natural inclination to fight with other roosters over territory and hens. Cockfighting roosters are specially bred to be strong and aggressive.

Before a cockfighting match, the birds' owners strap razor-sharp knives to the backs of their birds' legs. As the roosters jump up to peck and kick each other during a fight, the knives slash and maim their opponents. Eventually one bird is either dead or too injured to continue fighting, and the winner is

Cockfighting roosters are specially bred to be strong and aggressive.

declared. Spectators bet money on the outcome of the matches. Top fighting birds are very valuable as breeding animals to sire the next generation of competitors.

Cockfighting is a popular and legal sport in some countries, including Mexico, India, Thailand, and the Philippines. Cockfighting was also once widely practiced in the United States with George Washington and Thomas Jefferson among its notable participants. With the passage of a law banning cockfighting in Louisiana by August 2008, all fifty states have now made cockfighting illegal. However, banning the sport has not eliminated it. There is an extensive network of cockfighting fans that practice the sport in secret. Underground fighting is thought to be on the rise as more immigrants bring the cockfighting culture to their new homes in the United States. Laws against cockfighting are rarely enforced, and penalties are minimal. Participants who are caught receive only small fines. In Ohio, the penalty for cockfighting is the same as a speeding ticket.

The Humane Society of the United States (HSUS) has pushed for stronger penalties for those who break laws against cockfighting. "It's an indefensible form of staging fights—watching these animals hack each other to death. Any sensible person can see there is no socially redeeming aspect of cockfighting,"[44] says HSUS president Wayne Pacelle. Thirty-three states have made cockfighting a felony. In forty states it is illegal to be a spectator at a cockfight. But cockfighting is not usually considered a priority for law enforcement officials. "Prosecuting cockfighting is labor-intensive and costly. It's not productive to tie up your resources on it,"[45] says a deputy sheriff in Ohio.

The Chicken Police

"Why would any rational sheriff want to go out and arrest someone for going out and owning a chicken, with all the other things going on in the country?" —Jack Cairnes, cockfighting proponent.

Quoted in Jonathan Martin, "Cockfighting, Its Loyal Fans Keep Fighting to the Death," *Seattle Times*, March 11, 2007, p. B1.

Dogfighting

Another blood sport is dogfighting, and it is growing in popularity in the United States. Although illegal in most states since the 1860s, an underground culture of dogfighting has persisted, especially in southern states. A new culture of dogfighting is also on the rise in urban areas and is often associated with drug dealing, gambling, and other criminal activity related to gangs.

Traditional dogfighting is a highly organized activity run by professional breeders who invest a great deal of time and money on staging fights and developing generations of fighting dogs. The dogs used are usually hybrids of several breeds developed for fighting and are generally known as pit bulls. These dogs possess such a strong drive to fight that they will often fight to the death instead of backing down when injured or overpowered. Pit bulls are extremely loyal toward people, and this quality adds to their willingness to fight for their masters.

Pit bulls undergo extensive training to prepare for fights. They are forced to run on treadmills to build endurance, often with the dangling bait of a cat or rabbit to entice them to keep going. Their owners have them grasp animal hides hanging from poles to strengthen their jaws and make them wear heavy chains and weights around their necks to develop upper-body strength.

During competitions pairs of dogs are released into a pit, where they immediately attack one another. Matches usually end in under an hour either when one dog is too injured to continue fighting and quits or when one of the dogs is killed. Owners sometimes kill animals that quit by hanging, shooting, or electrocuting them. Top dogs are highly valued for both fighting and stud services and may fetch prices of up to twenty-five thousand dollars.

Leading the Way

"The U.S. is certainly one of the world leaders in trying to regulate inter-species dignity." —Colin Levey, columnist for the *Wall Street Journal*.

Colin Levey, *Wall Street Journal*, May 2, 2003, p. W13.

Dogfights that take place in urban areas are usually less organized. Known as street fighters, dogs used in these fights are not the result of carefully planned breeding and training. Instead owners buy dogs off the street and provoke them to become vicious by whipping them and burning them with cigarettes, resulting in dogs extremely quick to attack.

Because of its connection with other crime and most people's strong objection to cruelty against dogs, dogfighting is actively targeted by law enforcement. Participating in dogfighting is a felony in all states except Idaho and Montana, where it carries the lesser charge of a misdemeanor. In forty-six states it is also

In Afghanistan, dogfighting is a popular pastime, and matches are a weekly event.

illegal to be a spectator at dogfighting events. Dogfighters can also be charged under anticruelty laws. Penalties can include jail time and substantial fines. In 2004, one longtime South Carolina breeder was sentenced to thirty years in prison for his dogfighting activities.

Despite law enforcement efforts, dogfighting shows no sign of declining. The HSUS estimates that approximately forty thousand professional dogfighters operate in the United States. Another one hundred thousand are street fighters. "This dog fighting deal is right under our noses. It's a big deal . . . probably as big as the underworld drug business. It's everywhere,"[46] says a law enforcement official in Texas.

Prior to the sentencing of professional football quarterback Michael Vick on dogfighting charges in 2007, protesters expressed their outrage against all dogfighting.

Proponents of dogfighting defend their sport, saying it is not cruel because the dogs want to fight, even love to fight. Pit bull breeder Bill Stewart explains: "It's about two highly conditioned athletes going at each other with everything they have to try to win. It's the purest form of combat on earth."[47]

Rodeo

Most people agree that blood sports such as cockfighting and dogfighting promote animal cruelty and should be illegal. However, the cruelty of other legal sports involving animals is the subject of debate. One such sport is rodeo. Rodeo is a sport with origins in the roping and riding skills once commonly used by cowboys. Today rodeo has become big business in the United

States and Canada, with professional rodeo stars competing for millions of dollars in prize money.

Most fans view rodeo as wholesome family entertainment, but animal rights activists criticize many rodeo events. Critics claim that rodeo animals are subjected to cruel treatment during events such as bronco and bull riding as well as steer wrestling and calf roping. The Professional Rodeo Cowboys Association (PRCA) strongly disagrees with this claim. The organization says it has a thorough animal welfare policy in place for the treatment of animals in the rodeos it sanctions. It also requires that a veterinarian attend all events. Rodeo

Animal Actors

Hollywood has a long history of casting animals in movie and television roles. When the practice first began, little concern was given to the welfare of the animal actors. However, when a horse was killed after being ridden over a cliff during the filming of the movie *Jesse James* in 1939, there was great public outcry. As a result, in 1940 animal safety representatives from the American Humane Association were given the authority to monitor the welfare of animal actors. Eventually, the group developed a set of guidelines that is now used to safeguard animals used in any sort of filming, including movies, television, commercials, and music videos. Films that comply with all guidelines are awarded the ability to include the phrase, "No Animals Were Harmed" during their end credits.

Despite these safeguards, animal rights organizations object to the use of animal actors. They say that many trainers employ cruel practices to force animals to perform for the cameras. They are especially critical of the practice of using great apes, such as chimpanzees and orangutans, in the industry. Because of the strength and aggressive nature of these animals, activists claim that heavy-handed training methods are often required. They document many cases of punishment by beating or other cruel treatment. They also claim that many of these social animals are forced to endure solitary lives in small, cramped cages and spend long hours traveling. In addition, animal rights supporters condemn the action of taking these animals from their mothers during infancy in order to provide cute, young animals for filming. Because of these practices, People for the Ethical Treatment of Animals (PETA) and other animal rights organizations have called for an end to the use of apes in Hollywood.

organizers stress that it is in their economic interest to treat rodeo stock well. Rodeos contract with livestock owners who make large investments to provide the best performing animals possible. Abused and injured animals would perform poorly and cause their owners to earn less or go out of business entirely. Many bucking horses and bulls perform for years, becoming stars in their own right.

Rodeo opponents dispute that horses and bulls are well treated and point to several practices they believe are cruel. One is the use of flank straps placed around the abdomens of bulls and horses to encourage them to buck. Critics say the straps are painful and cause injury to the animals. The PRCA counters that flank straps do not cause pain. Instead, they say, the strap simply encourages the animal to kick its legs higher while bucking, resulting in a more dramatic performance by the rider.

The other rodeo event most often criticized is calf roping. In this event a rider on horseback throws a loop of rope around the neck of a running calf, pulling it to a rapid stop. The sudden jerk of the rope can cause injury to calves, including broken necks, backs, and limbs. To help minimize injuries, PRCA rules prohibit flipping or dragging the calf, but, even so, sometimes calves are hurt or killed.

ANIMAL ABUSE FOR ENTERTAINMENT

"It's animal abuse merchandised as family entertainment. . . . This is not family entertainment. How do you think kids feel when they see some little animal get its neck broken?" —Peggy Larson, veterinarian and former bronco rider, referring to rodeo.

Quoted in Claudia Rowe, "Pros and Cons of Rodeo Roping and Riding," *New York Times*, June 16, 2002, p. 14WC.6.

The PRCA keeps track of injuries to animals used in its rodeos. In 2001 they recorded twenty-five injuries out of 85,638 uses of animals—a .029 percent injury rate. Animal rights groups challenge these numbers and call on people to protest against rodeos when they come to town. The efforts of animal rights groups to prove rodeo animal abuse and shut down rodeos have so far been largely unsuccessful. PETA representative Amy Rhodes says, "We want rodeo out of business, but we know it's not going to happen overnight."[48]

Horse Racing

Another sport targeted by animal rights activists is horse racing. Thoroughbred horse racing, a multibillion-dollar industry, is the leading animal sport in the United States. Approximately ninety thoroughbred racetracks host over sixty thousand races each year. Occasionally a racehorse becomes a household name after a winning season, gaining the privilege of retiring to stud on a lavish breeding farm. For most horses, however, the racing life is not so glamorous.

Critics of horse racing point out the physical toll that training and racing has on the fragile bodies of these highly bred animals. Horses begin racing at age two when they are not yet fully mature. As a result, horses suffer frequent injuries to their delicate feet and legs. To keep them in competition, trainers and veterinarians may give painkilling drugs to horses with illnesses or injuries. Massive injuries, such as shattered leg bones, and even deaths are not uncommon during training or races. In fact, hundreds of racehorses die at tracks each year. "It's part of the game,"[49] says one jockey.

Recently, some famous racehorses have died from injuries suffered in the sport's most famous contests. In 2008 the second place finisher in the Kentucky Derby shattered both front ankles at the race's end and was euthanized. In 2006, after winning the Kentucky Derby, the colt Barbaro fractured his hind leg during the Preakness Stakes and was also eventually euthanized when the injury failed to heal.

Due to the great expense of buying, housing, feeding, and training racehorses, owners tend to treat their horses as investments, making decisions about their futures based on their earning potential. Winning horses can earn millions for their owners through prize money and stud fees. Losing horses, however, are sold or retired to adoptive owners. Many injured horses are euthanized so that the owners do not have to spend money on veterinary fees for an animal that has no future earning potential.

Critics point out that horse racing exists primarily to generate money through gambling. However, there are many people involved in racing who genuinely love and care for horses and admire their beauty and passion for running. Still, some question if the sport is justified. George Vecsey, a sportswriter for the *New York Times*, wonders, "These fragile thoroughbreds do not exactly have much say, other than demonstrating that they love to run. Perhaps that is why we love them and respect them and protect them, although not nearly enough, from the stress of

Barbaro, winner of the 2006 Kentucky Derby, pulls up lame with an injury to his right rear leg at the start of the Preakness Stakes at Pimlico Race Course in Baltimore. Despite multiple surgeries, Barbaro did not survive his broken leg.

Greyhound Racing

Another sport that draws heavy criticism from the animal rights community is greyhound racing. Those inside the greyhound-racing industry say that their animals are prized athletes that receive pet-quality care. In contrast, critics claim that dogs are sometimes the victims of poor treatment and housing conditions while in training or at the track. Most criticism, however, is focused on the huge surplus of animals produced by greyhound breeders in their quest for animals that will win races.

Many of the puppies born are not of racing quality and are killed in a process known as culling. In addition, greyhounds that perform poorly are retired and meet a variety of fates. Some are placed in adoptive family homes through programs managed by breeders and greyhound-rescue organizations. Others, however, are killed or sold to animal research facilities.

Greyhound racing peaked in the 1980s and early 1990s when a rapid expansion of tracks fueled a breeding frenzy. According to the Greyhound Protection League, in the twenty-one-year period from 1986 to 2006 over 180,000 young greyhounds were killed before they reached racing age. The Greyhound Protection League claims that over 24,000 greyhounds were born in 2006. Of these, about 1,600 puppies unfit for racing were culled. In that year nearly 15,000 retired greyhounds were adopted and nearly 7,000 others were killed.

Due to competition from other gambling opportunities such as casinos and poker halls, greyhound racing is on the decline. As of September 2007, there were thirty-five greyhound racing tracks operating in thirteen states, down from fifty-six tracks in 1990. Eight states have banned dog racing since 1993.

Many greyhound puppies that are born, but are not of racing quality, are killed in a process known as culling.

racing itself. After what we put them through, do we love them so much out of guilt?"⁵⁰

Under the Big Top

Another much-loved American tradition is a family visit to the circus to see trained animals perform. Animal rights activists, however, are sharply critical of animal acts in circuses, insisting that the elephants, big cats, primates, and other animals are forced to perform unnatural tricks through the use of abusive

Many animal rights activists are critical of circuses because they believe that abusive training tactics are used to get the animals to perform tricks, which can cause stress on the animals and may lead to violence.

training methods. Trainers have been accused of beating animals and employing electric prods to force animals to comply. Circus opponents also express concern over the mistreatment they say occurs when wild animals are forced to live in confinement during months on the road as they travel the country.

Joan Galvin, spokesperson for Ringling Bros. and Barnum & Bailey Circus responds to these accusations:

> Most reputable circuses have incredibly dedicated and professional staff. It's almost a personal affront to hear these things. That's hard when it's your livelihood, and it's not an easy livelihood. It's in our best interest to do what's right and to treat these animals almost like members of the family, almost sometimes better than you treat your own family.[51]

There have been instances when circus animals have escaped and caused damage and injury to people. During a Wisconsin performance in 2002, two elephants escaped a circus tent, with one of them injuring a boy before being brought under control. In 1994 an elephant killed its trainer and escaped the big top in Honolulu, rampaging through city streets before being shot by police. Circus critics point to these instances as signs of the stress circus animals are exposed to, saying mistreatment causes them to finally "snap." Other reported violations include an elephant dying from heatstroke while traveling and animals injured by mistreatment from trainers. "What all this is saying is that circuses are not always doing the best job there is or that they can do with these animals,"[52] says Richard Sarinato of the HSUS.

Despite the efforts of animal rights organizations to put an end to the use of animals in sports and entertainment, the public has continued to show strong support for these activities. Because many mainstream animal-related pursuits play such a prominent role in human culture, it is unlikely that they will end any time soon. However, by exposing some of the hidden aspects of animal cruelty sometimes associated with these practices, animal rights activists are playing a role in improving the welfare of the animals involved.

Animal Rights and Wildlife

Many people disagree over the use of animals for food, research, and entertainment. However, more people share concerns regarding the treatment of free-living wild animals. The practice of hunting wild animals for food, fur, and trophies has become increasingly controversial in many parts of the world. Throughout the past several decades, animal rights groups have mounted a wide variety of campaigns aimed at influencing the public's attitude toward these activities in an effort to bring an end to practices they believe are both cruel and immoral. Some of these efforts seem to be working. Fewer people today than in previous decades support wearing animal fur and hunting animals for trophies.

A Hunting Tradition

The viewpoint that there should be limitations on people's use of wild animals is a relatively recent development in human history. Primitive humans began hunting wild animals over a million years ago. Many human traits, such as the ability to communicate, work cooperatively, and carefully observe the environment through sights and sounds, strongly influenced early humans' success as hunters. In fact, according to author Richard Bulliet, "Hunting gave rise to the distinctive characteristics of humankind. Hunting is an inborn and indelible human trait."[53]

Even after people began relying on agriculture to provide food, hunting was still a very common practice for obtaining meat to eat and gaining hides and fur for making clothing. In a few places hunting remains the primary method for acquiring food, such as in Inuit communities in the Arctic, where the climate makes agriculture impossible. Many animal rights organizations do not have objections to hunting when it is necessary for providing for the daily needs of people. This type of hunting is called subsistence hunting. Today, however, hunting in the United States is rarely viewed as a necessity and is usually considered a recreational activity. Although many hunters still consume the animals they kill, most participate in the sport for the thrill of the hunt and the opportunity to enjoy time in nature with family and friends.

An Emotional Experience

"Part of what makes hunting such an intensely emotional experience is the physical responsibility you take for the death of your food." —Margaret Knox, author.

Quoted in James A. Swan, *In Defense of Hunting*. San Francisco: HarperSanFrancisco, 1995, p. 239.

In recent decades animal rights groups have begun to condemn hunting as a nonessential activity in the modern world. "Although it was a crucial part of humans' survival 100,000 years ago, hunting is now nothing more than a violent form of recreation that the vast majority of hunters does not need for subsistence,"[54] claims PETA. Some people, such as deer hunter George N. Wallace, question if hunting still has a place as wilderness regions decline, affording wildlife fewer opportunities for sanctuary:

> The more we eliminate the wet and wild places from our farms and ranches, the more we dice and cut, spreading our homes and business deals over first the farms, then the hills above them, along the lake shores and streams and into the forest, the less we will be able, in good faith, to pick up the shotgun or rifle to take to the fields that are left. Even if we do find a few derelict patches that look healthy, we must know that the game we seek is cut off and more vulnerable to our presence now. We must wonder, at some point, if we still have the right.[55]

Along with hunting for food, many hunters participate in the sport because they enjoy spending time in nature with family and friends.

In the United States alone, hunters kill about 200 million animals each year, including 4 million deer, 12 million ducks and geese, 25 million rabbits and squirrels, and 21,000 black bears. Some of the strongest objections to hunting are aimed at practices viewed as particularly unsporting—when animals are given virtually no chance of escape. Some of these activities include the use of high-tech tools to attract and kill animals; baiting bears with food so that hiding hunters can shoot them; chasing bears, bobcats, and mountain lions into trees with dogs; and hunting wolves and other predators from helicopters. Other concerns are the suffering of wounded animals that escape and the impact that the fear and stress of the chase has on the ability of the animals to feed, travel, and rest.

Does Hunting Contribute to Conservation?

Supporters of hunting counter that instead of harming animals, their activities actually help conserve wildlife populations and habitats. Legally hunted game species are carefully managed by state wildlife agencies that strictly regulate the number of each type of animal killed. Fees from hunting and fishing licenses and taxes from ammunition, guns, and other gear provide 75 percent of the financial support for all state fish and wildlife management programs, totaling over $745 million annually. Through the years this money has also funded the establishment of over 4,000 state wildlife areas encompassing 45 million acres (18 million ha) that also provide recreational opportunities to nonhunters. Through hunter-supported conservation efforts, populations

Killing for Conservation

Sometimes hunting is used as a management method to help save endangered species or habitats. From the Channel Islands off the coast of California to Ecuador's Galapagos Islands, hunting is used as a conservation tool. Both of these island chains, as well as many others around the world, have suffered from the effects of nonnative animals destroying plant communities or preying on rare species. Pigs, goats, rats, deer, and other animals have been introduced to these places both accidentally and on purpose. In these fragile island environments, the presence of new animals can have devastating effects on plants and animals that have evolved in isolation. In some cases, the populations of these introduced animals have grown so large that they overwhelm the native environment. Rats and pigs eat the eggs and chicks of rare birds, while goats and deer eat the plants, reducing food for native grazers and driving plants to extinction.

Conservationists have turned to hunting as a means of controlling these wildlife pests. They wage campaigns against the intruders by poisoning, trapping, and hunting with dogs or from helicopters. Many animal rights groups strongly protest this killing. Critics believe the hunting methods are cruel and say that saving one species does not justify the killing of another. They instead propose capturing and sterilizing animals to control their populations. Wildlife managers say such programs are extremely expensive and are usually not effective.

of many game species that were once in decline have made notable comebacks. For example, in the 1920s there were 300,000 white-tailed deer, 30,000 wild turkeys, and 50,000 elk in the United States. Now those populations stand at 20 million deer, 4.5 million turkeys, and 1 million elk.

In addition to pointing to their contributions to wildlife conservation, pro-hunting organizations such as the National Rifle Association (NRA) also take the stance that most hunters possess a deep respect and reverence for nature. They are angered by

Pro-hunting activist and rock musician Ted Nugent displays his bow-hunting skills at the state capitol in Lansing, Michigan.

the campaigns of animal rights groups that portray hunters as unfeeling killers who care nothing about wildlife. Most hunters, these organizations insist, have a deep sense of connection and commitment to the land.

Supporters of hunting also strongly assert their right to continue their pastime based on human biology and cultural traditions and object to animal rights groups' forcing their values on society. "Sustaining life at the expense of other life is what makes this planet function, and humans are a part of that system,"[56] says Jim Posewitz, founder of a pro-hunting organization. The NRA states, "Whether it's for companionship or solitude, to commune or participate with nature, the challenge or tradition, or perhaps just a fondness for wild meat, hunting remains as it should always remain, a personal choice."[57] H. Dale Hall, director of the U.S. Fish and Wildlife Service (USFWS), is even more forceful in his opinion. Hunting, he says, is "not just a freedom here, it's a right."[58]

Hunting Profits Support Wildlife

"Hunters were the first conservationists." —The National Rifle Association.

The National Rifle Association, "What Hunters' Dollars Buy." www.nrahq.org/hunting/huntdollarsbuy.asp.

Declining Participation

Whether a result of antihunting campaigns by animal rights advocates or simply a reflection of changing times, participation in hunting has been declining since the middle of the twentieth century. A survey conducted by the USFWS showed that only 12.5 million people, or 5 percent of the U.S. population, hunted in 2006. This is a 4 percent decline from 2001. In addition, the population of hunters is aging, with fewer young people taking up the sport.

While interest in hunting appears to be fading, other wildlife-related recreation is increasing. The USFWS poll showed that 31 percent of Americans engaged in wildlife watching such as

Do Fish Feel Pain?

While most animal rights campaigns focus on creatures that are furry, cute, and cuddly, in recent years activists have begun voicing concern over the treatment of a surprising group of animals—fish. Most people give little consideration to the idea that fishing causes pain and suffering, but new research may change that perception. A team of biologists in Scotland conducted a series of experiments to discover whether fish could feel pain. First, they examined the nervous system of trout and determined that they have the same type of specialized nerve endings around their mouths that people do. Next, the researchers stimulated the nerve endings by injecting bee venom under the skin and observed the trout's behavior. The fish acted in ways that the biologists interpreted as feelings of pain: Their gills beat faster, they rubbed their irritated skin on the walls of the tank, and they stopped eating.

Although research indicates that fish feel pain, does that mean that fish hooked on a line actually experience suffering? It is a much more difficult question to determine whether fish have the mental capacity to actually feel emotion and suffer. However, studies of the brains of fish indicate that the areas associated with emotion, learning, and memory are similar to those of mammal brains.

bird-watching or wildlife photography in 2006, an 8 percent increase from 2001.

Although most Americans do not hunt, not everyone opposes the activity. Another USFWS poll showed that 70 percent of people approve of hunting wild animals for food. However, only 25 percent support hunting for sport.

The public's increasing intolerance of sport hunting and declining interest in hunting have many advocates concerned. The NRA and other hunting organizations have developed special programs to attract young people and women to the sport. Even so, the general view is that "hunting in America has entered a long twilight."[59] According to Cornell University researchers studying hunting trends, "Certainly without, and perhaps even with, extraordinary intervention efforts on a scale we've never seen before, hunting is going to continue to decline over the foreseeable future."[60]

Trophy Hunting

Perhaps the practice least understood and most often opposed by the nonhunting public is trophy hunting. Trophy hunters pursue the largest, most exotic, and most rare creatures to kill in order to display their mounted bodies or enter their feats in hunting record books. Trophy hunters are usually wealthy individuals who may spend tens of thousands of dollars traveling to remote locations and hiring hunting guides to lead them to their prey, such as polar bears, lions, elephants, zebras, and giraffes.

Animal rights advocates condemn the practice of trophy hunting outright. Says Wayne Pacelle of the HSUS:

> It's a perverse and destructive subculture. Thousands of animals suffer and die for the amusement of wealthy elites who have the means to pursue any form of recreation, but choose to shoot the world's rarest and most beautiful animals. There's no societal value to the exercise, just a selfish all-consuming mentality of killing, collecting, and showing off trophies. They know the price of every animal, but the value of none.[61]

It's Murder

"Did the fact that [serial killer] Jeffrey Dahmer ate his victims justify his crimes? What is done with a corpse after its murder doesn't lessen the victim's suffering." —PETA.

PETA, "Wildlife FAQs." www.peta.org/about/faq-wild.asp.

Supporters of trophy hunting say that the large sums of money they spend to bag their prizes support conservation by encouraging local people to protect wildlife for its economic value. Some African governments have created limited hunting opportunities, allowing people to shoot even some of their endangered wildlife, in an effort to raise money and boost local employment.

One of the strongest advocates of trophy hunting is the organization Safari Club International (SCI). SCI maintains a record book that details hunting statistics of thousands of trophy animals taken over the last one hundred years. The organization presents annual awards to members for their most impressive hunting achievements. Former SCI president John J. Jackson III explains his view of trophy hunting: "A trophy of any species attests that its owner has been somewhere and done something, that he has exercised skilled persistence and discrimination in the agile feat of overcoming, outwitting, and reducing game to possession."[62]

One of the most controversial methods of trophy hunting is that which takes place on private, fenced hunting ranches both abroad and in the United States. There are estimated to be over one thousand private game reserves in the United States. Many

Two men display a black Hawaiian sheep, killed during a "canned hunt" of captive, exotic animals on a private Oregon game reserve.

of these ranches provide hunters with the opportunity to pay to hunt native and exotic animals living in the reserve. Because many of these animals have become accustomed to humans and are confined by fences, these hunts have become known as "canned hunts."

While popular with some hunters willing to pay for a guaranteed trophy, canned hunts are increasingly criticized by both animal rights advocates and members of the hunting community. Many hunters condemn the practice for eliminating the concept of "fair chase" that tests a hunter's skill and gives the animal the chance to escape. Jim Posewitz, president of a sport hunting organization explains: "Fundamental to ethical hunting is the idea of fair chase. This concept addresses the balance between the hunter and the hunted. It is a balance that allows hunters to occasionally succeed while animals generally avoid being taken."[63]

Fur for Fashion

Another controversial use of wildlife as a human resource is the killing of animals to provide fur for the fashion industry. More than 50 million mink, chinchillas, foxes, coyotes, lynx, beavers, and other wild animals are harvested for their fur every year. The majority of fur is produced on fur farms. On these farms, animals are housed in an extremely confined manner similar to factory farms that raise domestic animals for food.

Fur is also obtained by trapping animals living in the wild. Trappers use snares, underwater traps, and leg-hold traps to catch their prey. This method of hunting wild animals—especially the use of leg-hold traps—is strongly criticized by animal rights groups because of the high degree of pain and suffering it can cause animals. Animals caught in leg-hold traps usually suffer severe crushing injuries to the trapped limb. In its frantic struggle to free itself, an animal may chew or twist off its own leg. Eventually the animal becomes exhausted and may die of exposure and shock or may wait trapped for several days until the trapper returns to kill it. Because leg-hold traps cannot select their targets, they claim many accidental victims, including dogs and cats and other nontargeted wildlife. Several states

Calling Off the Hounds

Animal rights organizations claimed victory in 2004 when the British government banned the sport of foxhunting with dogs in England and Wales. For centuries, people have ridden horses behind packs of foxhounds as they followed the scent of foxes. A successful hunt ended as the hounds caught and killed their fox. According to animal rights activists who criticized the hunt, the fox's death was extremely inhumane as the pack of dogs ripped the living animal into pieces. Fox hunters disagreed. They claimed the fox would usually be killed by a single bite from one of the hounds.

As the new law took effect in early 2005, many members of foxhunting clubs condemned the action and staged vocal protests. Some even threatened to defy the ban. To them, hunting foxes with hounds is an age-old tradition that bonds members of the community. In addition, foxes are considered pest animals in rural Britain; hunts helped farmers rid their fields of the livestock predators. Under the new law, Britain's quarter of a million foxes may still be killed by shooting, poisoning, or catching in snares. Only the act of chasing and catching foxes by packs of dogs is prohibited.

Since being banned, traditional foxhunts have been replaced by "drag" hunts. In a drag hunt, a trail of fox scent is laid across the countryside. While most traditional hunters prefer the real thing, these new hunts will provide opportunities for hunters to continue exercising their dogs and horses.

In 2004, the British government banned the sport of foxhunting with dogs in England and Wales.

and cities have banned the use of leg-hold traps because of safety and humane concerns.

Because of publicity about the condition animals face on fur farms and the suffering experienced by animals captured in the trapping industry, the wearing of fur is now much less accepted by the public than it was a few decades ago. Many clothing designers and retailers, especially in the United States and the United Kingdom, have adopted a fur-free policy for their products in response to pressure from both their customers and animal rights groups.

But not all fur suppliers have adopted this policy. In the early 1970s, animal rights groups began displaying images of blood-covered ice and hunters clubbing baby seals. This resulted in a huge public outcry that led to a ban on imports of seal products to the United States in 1972. Despite the end of a market for seal pelts in the United States, seal hunters continue to harvest animals in northeastern Canada and sell their furs in other parts of

Although the Canadian government says that most seals are killed quickly and humanely, animal rights groups say that during a seal hunt, young seals scream in fear as hunters club nearby animals, and many are skinned while still alive.

the world, such as China, Russia, and the European Union (which in early 2008 was debating a seal product ban of its own).

The Canadian government establishes the number of seals that it will allow to be killed. This number is called a quota and varies from year to year based on the size of the seal population. To maintain a desired population size of 4.07 million harp seals, the government allowed a quota of 335,000 in 2006 and 270,000 in 2007. Government spokespersons say that most seals are killed quickly and that hunters follow humane regulations to ensure that the animals do not suffer.

Keeping Hunters Away

"Protective of bunnies and Bambis, suburbanites increasingly restrict hunting from getting anywhere near their mini-mansions." —Steve Tuttle, general editor of *Newsweek*.

Steve Tuttle, "The Elusive Hunter," *Newsweek*, December 4, 2006. www.newsweek.com/id/43951/.

Animal rights groups counter that the seal hunt is far from humane. For one, they say, young seals left on the ice by their mothers are unable to escape and scream in fear as hunters club nearby animals. They also claim that seals are commonly skinned while still alive. And animal rights groups worry that the seal population cannot sustain such a hunt. They say quotas are often exceeded, as many wounded seals drown and are unaccounted for in the numbers killed. Plus, as ice floes shrink due to global climate change, a lower survival rate for newborn seals might result.

Supporters of the seal hunt disagree. They say that the hunt is strictly monitored to ensure quotas are not exceeded. They argue that seal hunting is a Canadian tradition that dates back hundreds of years and is an important part of the region's economy. Phil Jenkins, a spokesperson for the Canadian Department of Fisheries and Oceans responds to criticism from animal rights groups:

> I think the reason that this is controversial is the emotion that is brought in to the debate. Humans eat meat,

use animal products, but they rarely see the process of killing animals. The seal hunt happens in open sight on white ice. These are powerful visual images and these organizations that are opposed to the hunt use an emotional approach and misrepresent the facts.[64]

Animal rights groups are not swayed by this argument and object to what they consider cruelty solely for the production of unessential luxury items. They have called on consumers to boycott Canadian seafood until the hunting stops. The HSUS claims that polls show that nearly 70 percent of Canadians support a ban on commercial seal hunting. Says Paul Watson of the animal rights group Sea Shepherd, "The war against the Canadian seal hunt is more than a protest. It is a crusade to bring about harmony between the natural world and humanity. All of us who oppose it are dedicated to the protection of life and the abolition of cruelty."[65]

While the Canadian government may present arguments supporting the hunt for traditional and economic reasons, Rebecca Aldworth, director of Canadian wildlife issues for the HSUS says, "At the end of the day it's still the largest slaughter of marine mammals in the world."[66]

Hunting Great Whales

Seals are not the only marine mammals targeted by hunters. Commercial whalers have heavily hunted the great whales, such as blue, gray, right, and sperm whales, since the 1900s. This hunting decimated great whale populations, pushing many species to the edge of extinction. Recognizing the harmful impact of intensive commercial whaling, the International Whaling Commission (IWC) enacted an indefinite ban, known as a moratorium, on commercial whaling in 1986. This moratorium is supported by nearly all of the IWC's, seventy-eight member nations.

The countries of Japan, Norway, and Iceland, however, object to the moratorium and continue commercial whaling. Norway and Iceland conduct their whaling activities in the North Atlantic. They claim the hunt provides its citizens an opportunity to eat whale meat, a cultural tradition in those countries.

Even though the International Whaling Commission enacted an indefinite ban on commercial whaling in 1986, Japan, Norway, and Iceland objected and continued their commercial whaling activities.

Critics, however, claim the market for whale meat there has nearly disappeared. The antiwhaling organization Greenpeace claims that meat from Iceland's recent catches of endangered fin whales was discarded. Norway ended its 2006 whale hunt early, catching only 444 minke whales out of their planned hunt of 1,000 animals. Norwegian officials say the hunt was called off due to bad weather and the poor quality of the year's whale meat. However, critics of the whale hunt say the real reason was lack of demand for the meat.

Japan carries out its hunt in the North Pacific and the Antarctic's Southern Ocean Whale Sanctuary, claiming to do so for scientific research purposes, an activity legally allowed under the moratorium. According to Japan, their harvest of hundreds of whales each year provides data about whales, such as what they eat and how long they live. This information, they claim, will allow better management of whale and fishery resources. The Institute of Cetacean Research, a whale research organization authorized by the Japanese government, explains: "The purpose of Japan's whale research is to gather scientific data required to establish a management regime for the sustainable use of whale resources. For this purpose some indispensable data have to be collected by lethal means, which simply cannot be obtained by non-lethal means."[67]

Antiwhaling animal rights groups scoff at the notion of "scientific" whaling. Because the whale meat is sold to restaurants and supermarkets, says Greenpeace, "the commercial nature of Japan's whaling operation is undeniable."[68] For the 2007 whaling season, Japan planned to hunt a total of 1,035 whales—935 minkes, 50 endangered fin, and 50 endangered humpbacks—for scientific purposes in the Southern Ocean Whale Sanctuary alone. International public outcry, however, caused them to abandon their plans to kill humpbacks.

Greenpeace argues that whales do not need to be killed to be studied. Modern wildlife research techniques such as satellite tracking and individual identification of animals makes killing unnecessary. "Japan's whalers are deceiving the Japanese public by painting the word 'research' on their ships," says Junichi Sato of Greenpeace. "Real scientists don't need to kill whales to study them. This is commercial whaling poorly dressed up as science."[69]

Already at Risk

"Three hundred thousand whales and dolphins drown in fishing nets each year and it is impossible to calculate how many more fall victim to pollution, ship strikes, the impacts of sonar or climate change. How can pro-whaling nations justify hunting them as well?" —Karen Sack, Greenpeace USA whales project leader.

Quoted in Greenpeace, "Threats to Whales and Dolphins Highlighted Around the World on Eve of Whaling Commission Meeting in Alaska." www.greenpeace.org/usa/press-center/releases2/threats-to-whales-and-dolphins.

Animal rights activists object to commercial whale hunting for a variety of reasons. They, and many wildlife biologists, believe that populations of whales still recovering from the intensive hunting of earlier decades are not yet large enough to sustain

Hunting Dolphins in Japan

While most countries have outlawed the hunting of dolphins and whales, this practice continues in a handful of countries. Each year several small towns on the coast of Japan conduct a hunt of dolphins and pilot whales. Fishers use nets and loud noises to herd the animals into shallow bays where they are stabbed with knives. The waters of the bays turn red as the animals bleed to death. Afterward the dolphins that are killed are sold for fertilizer, pet food, or food for humans. Some dolphins are captured alive and sold to aquariums for display.

This hunting practice has caused outrage from governments, animal rights organizations, and wildlife biologists from all over the world. "The Japanese dolphin drive hunts are an astonishingly cruel violation of any reasonable animal welfare standards. . . . In the case of dolphins, who share many cognitive and emotional characteristics with our own species, it is an unconscionable act of violence that has no place in a civilized society," say Diana Reiss and Lori Marino, authors of a scientific paper condemning the practice.

The government of Japan defends the hunt and considers it an important cultural tradition. Despite criticism, it allows the practice to continue. Government officials also claim that the dolphins are killed to prevent competition with local fishing enterprises, although critics claim that there is no proof that the dolphins have an impact on fisheries.

The Institute of Cetacean Research, "Japan's Research Whaling in the Arctic." www.icrwhale.org/QandA Research.htm.

hunting. In addition, other environmental factors such as pollution, ocean noise, fishing nets, collisions with ships, and global warming already place whale populations under enormous pressure. Finally, opponents of whaling also consider the practices employed to kill whales to be extremely inhumane. Whales shot by cannon-driven harpoons often take many minutes to die. It is thought that whales experience a great deal of distress and suffering as they are pursued and killed.

Like many animal rights issues, whaling and the killing of other wildlife is a highly emotional issue that includes many different points of view. The variety of cultures, traditions, and values that impact these issues almost certainly guarantee that the debate will continue.

The Tactics of Animal Rights Activists: Do They Go Too Far?

The treatment of animals by people is an emotionally charged issue. Most people, quite understandably, react with shock and disgust to photos and descriptions of animals that suffer from mistreatment and abuse. Animal rights groups have capitalized on the compassionate feelings most people have toward animals. Many have become highly adept at developing messages and creating sensational media events and slogans that use emotion.to generate support for their point of view.

Animal rights organizations are so skilled at delivering their messages that many of their ideas and practices have become widely accepted. This fact concerns those who believe that the general public fails to grasp the true motives of the animal rights movement. Writer and ethicist Wesley J. Smith explains:

> We need to look past the public image of animal-rights/liberation groups, such as the People for the Ethical Treatment of Animals (PETA), as committed animal lovers who engage in wacky advocacy tactics such as posing nude to protest fur. For beneath this relatively benign façade lurks an ideologically absolutist movement that explicitly espouses equal moral worth between humans and animals. What's wrong with wanting to protect animals? Absolutely nothing. Indeed, advocating for animal welfare can be a noble cause. But this isn't the ultimate agenda of animal rights/liberation.[70]

Messages and Tactics

The ultimate agenda of animal rights groups is not always apparent. Most people are unaware that these groups believe that animals and people should be considered equals. Ingrid Newkirk, cofounder and president of PETA, illustrated this viewpoint when she once famously stated, "There is no rational basis for saying that a human being has special rights. A rat is a pig is a dog is a boy."[71] Many animal rights groups also believe that every human use of animals should end, including the keeping of pets.

Rights Are for Humans

"Rights are moral principles governing the interactions of rational, productive beings, who prosper not in a world of eat or be eaten, but a world of voluntary, mutually beneficial cooperation and trade." —Alex Epstein, philosopher opposed to granting rights to animals.

Alex Epstein, "The 'Animal Rights' Movement's Cruelty to Human Well-Being," *New York Beacon*, August 25–31, 2005, p. 23.

Of all the organizations advancing an extreme animal rights agenda, none has a higher profile than PETA. In 2004 the nonprofit organization received nearly $30 million in donations supporting its animal rights campaigns. PETA's many Web sites contain information on every facet of the human use of animals and are viewed by more than 30 million people each year. PETA heavily targets children and teens through specialized Web sites and other materials that promote their messages, often using sensational slogans, celebrity endorsements, and giveaways that appeal to youth.

While PETA's campaigns may be popular with young people, their methods and those of other animal rights advocates, which attempt to force others to adhere to their beliefs, are often off-putting. In fact, many people connected to animal industries, as well as scientists, educators, and the general public, are concerned by the statements and tactics used by some of these

The Tactics of Animal Rights Activists

Ingrid Newkirk, cofounder and president of People for the Ethical Treatment of Animals (PETA), speaks at a news conference in 2006.

groups to promote animal rights. One concern is that their positions are often seen as favoring animals over people. For example, when asked what PETA's response would be if a cure for AIDS was discovered through animal testing, Newkirk replied, "We'd be against it."[72] Chris DeRose, founder of Last Chance for Animals, said, "If the death of one rat cured all diseases, it wouldn't make any difference to me."[73]

Additionally, animal rights campaigns employ a variety of tactics to bring publicity to what they say are cases of animal abuse.

In his book, *Animal Rights: The Inhumane Crusade*, animal rights critic Daniel T. Oliver claims that organizations may use unidentified or even fake photographs to portray cruelty to animals at the hands of trappers, farmers, or research scientists. Oliver notes that another tactic is to portray isolated cases of animal mistreatment as typical throughout an industry. An additional approach is to make unsubstantiated or false claims of abuse to smear the reputations of people and businesses that conduct animal-related activities with which they disagree. Oliver says:

> Animal rights organizations make constant allegations of animal abuse to attract media coverage, bring supporters into the movement, and raise funds. They target an increasingly urban population that has little direct experience with farm animals or wildlife and little understand-

A Researcher's Perspective

Over many years Edythe London, a professor and researcher at the University of California, Los Angeles, School of Medicine, has witnessed her colleagues facing harassment and threats by animal rights advocates. After a newspaper account of her research using primates to better understand and treat nicotine addiction in teenagers was published, she became a target herself. Members of the Animal Liberation Front broke a window in her home and flooded the interior with a garden hose, causing tens of thousands of dollars in damage. London expresses her frustration over these kinds of tactics aimed at discouraging researchers who use animals in their studies:

I have devoted my career to understanding how nicotine, methamphetamine and other drugs can hijack brain chemistry and leave the affected individual at the mercy of his or her addiction. . . . Thousands of other scientists use laboratory animals in other research, giving hope to those afflicted with a wide variety of ailments. We must not allow these extremists to stop important research that advances the human condition.

Edythe London, "Why I Use Animals in My Research: A UCLA Scientist Targeted by Animal Rights Activists Justifies her Work," *Los Angeles Times*, November 1, 2007, p. A27.

ing of the importance of animals in biomedical research. . . . Many of these allegations cannot be substantiated, and others are simply false. Moreover, their aim is dishonest: animal rights groups often say they want to improve animal treatment, but their actual goal is to end animal use and ownership.[74]

Cultivating Outrage

PETA seems to deliberately design campaign messages with high shock value to garner publicity, even if that publicity is negative. For two years in 2003 and 2004, PETA toured college campuses and other venues with an exhibit promoting a vegetarian lifestyle. The campaign, called "Holocaust on Your Plate," argued that eating meat and wearing leather were morally the same as the murder of millions of Jews during the Holocaust. To make their point, PETA compared photos of chickens kept in factory farm cages to starving inmates of German concentration camps. Other images and exhibit text compared slaughtered animals to murdered Jews.

These comparisons caused outrage, especially among the Jewish community. "The effort by PETA to compare the deliberate, systematic murder of millions of Jews to the issue of animal rights is abhorrent,"[75] fumed the Anti-Defamation League. Ethicist Wesley Smith agreed: "That PETA can't distinguish between the unspeakable evil of the Shoah [the Holocaust] and animal husbandry reveals a perverted sense of moral values that is almost beyond comprehension,"[76] he said.

Eventually PETA issued a lukewarm apology for the exhibit, but went on to offend again the next year. This time the exhibit, "Animal Liberation," compared the plight of animals to human slavery. Ads displayed images of the shackled foot of a black man next to that of a chained elephant. Another equated a seal being clubbed to a black civil rights protestor being beaten. One more compared a murdered black man with a cow in a slaughterhouse. The display toured seventeen cities in 2005 before it was suspended due to public outcry.

"There is no comparison between criminal lynchings and the legal butchering of animals for food. There is no comparison

An Activist's Perspective

The position we hold—the abolitionist position—is often said to be "extreme," and those of us who hold it are said to be "extremists." The unspoken suggestions are that extreme positions cannot be right, and that extremists must be wrong.

But I am an extremist when it comes to rape—I am against it all the time. I am an extremist when it comes to child abuse—I am against it all the time. I am an extremist when it comes to sexual discrimination, racial discrimination—I am against it all the time. I am an extremist when it comes to abuse to the elderly—I am against it all the time.

The plain fact is, moral truth often is extreme, and must be, for when the injustice is absolute, then one must oppose it—absolutely. And the injustice of vivisection is absolute.

Tom Regan, "The Torch of Reason, the Sword of Justice," speech given on World Day for Lab Animals, Westwood, CA, 1988. www.animalliberationfront.com/Philosophy/torch_of_reason.htm.

---

between slaves and animals,"[77] said the National Association for the Advancement of Colored People, condemning the exhibit. PETA spokesperson Dawn Carr defended their approach. "Every time you're challenging the status quo people will be upset. . . . There is no question that the exhibits are difficult to look at. . . . But it needs to be that way in order to break through the prejudice that exists," she said. "The purpose of this campaign is to point out that oppression and prejudice in any form is wrong."[78]

Not everyone disapproved of PETA's Animal Liberation campaign message. In an online poll, Terry Jones, a resident of Washington, D.C., responded positively about the exhibit:

> If you note the way people use animals, we are enslaving them. We take them out of their natural habitats and use them for our own personal gain. Horses weren't put on Earth to carry 115-pound jockies [jockeys] in the Kentucky Derby. Rare birds weren't placed here to have their precious wings clipped and put in cages. All of these examples sound just like what the Anglos did to the Africans during slavery.[79]

Tactics Turn Violent

Because some of the more extreme supporters of animal rights believe that the use of animals by people equates to slavery and murder, they justify the use of radical tactics to promote their views. In some cases these tactics are not just controversial, they are illegal. Increasingly, animal research facilities, animal researchers, and animal agriculture facilities are becoming the targets of vandalism, harassment, and even threats of violence and death. Most of these activities are carried out by people working in a loose network of underground activists, often under the banner of the Animal Liberation Front (ALF).

The ALF began in the United Kingdom in the 1970s and started operations in the United States in the 1980s. It now has operatives working in twenty countries. According to the ALF Web site, their movement "carries out direct action against

Extreme animal rights supporters often use violence to express their views. Shown here is the aftermath of the bombing of a Michigan State University mink research lab by the Animal Liberation Front (ALF) in 1992.

animal abuse in the form of rescuing animals and causing financial loss to animal exploiters, usually through the damage and destruction of property."[80] ALF's actions are undertaken by individuals working alone or in small, loosely organized groups targeting anyone they feel abuses or exploits animals. Actions have included the release of animals, theft, arson, and vandalism at animal research facilities, research animal breeding farms, and farms raising animals for the fur industry.

> ## Violent Activism
>
> "Animal rights activists engage in significant violence and lawlessness to coerce society into accepting their values."
> —Wesley J. Smith, an attorney and author critical of animal rights extremists.
>
> Wesley J. Smith, "Four Legs Good, Two Legs Bad: The Anti-Human Values of 'Animal Rights,'" *Human Life Review*, Winter 2007, p. 7.

The number and severity of attacks by ALF supporters and other extreme animal rights groups have risen dramatically in recent years. A report compiled by the Foundation for Biomedical Research in Washington, D.C., found that worldwide there were 88 incidents in the 1980s, 132 in the 1990s, and 363 incidents from 2000 to 2005. These attacks represent millions of dollars in property damage. The threat of animal rights–related violence has grown so severe that the FBI calls it "one of today's most serious domestic terrorism threats."[81]

These radical activists conduct long-term campaigns of intimidation and threats against their targets. One such target was Ed Walsh, a scientist using cats to study treatments for deafness at Boys Town National Research Hospital in Omaha, Nebraska. Walsh and his family were harassed through hundreds of phone calls and letters, had their home and office picketed, and even received a death threat aimed at their son. As a result, he ended his research.

> I can tell you that it was huge, devastating. It's a life-altering experience to have your life, and the lives of

your children, so exposed. Routine daily habits —like turning an ignition switch or walking across a parking lot—can become anxiety-ridden. . . . It was our hope to contribute fundamentally to solving the congenital deafness problem in children around the world. We will never know where the work might have gone.[82]

Scientists working at the University of California, Los Angeles, (UCLA) have also been repeatedly targeted. In one case a bomb aimed at a researcher studying primate behavior was left at the wrong house. Although it failed to explode, it was powerful enough to have destroyed the home, occupied by a seventy-year-old woman. In another case, UCLA neurobiology professor Dario Ringach announced his decision to halt his primate research after years of threats to his family. Ringach sent an e-mail to the ALF saying, "You win. Effective immediately, I am no longer doing animal research."[83]

The Challenge

"Will we rise to the challenge and prove our capacity for genuine altruism by ending our ruthless exploitation of the species in our power, not because we are forced to do so by rebels or terrorists, but because we recognize that our position is morally indefensible?" —Peter Singer, philosopher whose book, *Animal Liberation*, significantly influenced the formation of the modern animal rights movement.

Peter Singer, *Animal Liberation*. New York: New York Review, 1975, p. 248.

Jerry Vlasak, who operates the Animal Liberation Press Office, applauds the tactics that led to Ringach's announcement. "I think Dario Ringach is a poster boy for the concept that the use of force or the threat of force is an effective means to stop people who abuse animals."[84] Vlasak serves as a spokesperson for the ALF, operating a Web site that lists ALF targets and issuing press releases that detail the illegal actions of activists who work under the ALF banner. Vlasak works in the open and says he does not know any of the activists personally. However, his views are just as extreme. "Anyone fighting for their own liberation has had to use violence at some stage of the struggle, and I don't think animal independence is any different,"[85] he says. According to Vlasak, even murder would be justified for their cause. In a 2004 interview he spoke about animal researchers, saying, "I don't think you'd have to kill too many. I think for five lives, 10 lives, 15 human lives, we could save a million, 2 million, 10 million nonhuman lives."[86]

The Huntingdon Life Sciences Case

One of the most high-profile, far-reaching, and long-term targets of the animal rights' radical fringe was Huntingdon Life Sciences (HLS), a company that conducts product-safety tests on animals. In 1999 a group called Stop Huntingdon Animal Cruelty (SHAC) began attacks against the company's facilities and staff in the United Kingdom and later also targeted its New Jersey lab. While some of their efforts attacked HLS directly, many more were directed at Huntingdon's staff members personally. Over the course of several years, SHAC members vandalized HLS staff members' cars, spray painted graffiti on their homes, threw rocks though their windows, and delivered death threats.

Whatever Means Necessary

"I think people who torture innocent beings should be stopped. If they won't stop when you ask them nicely, they don't stop when you demonstrate to them what they're doing is wrong, then they should be stopped using whatever means necessary."
—Dr. Jerry Blasak, Animal Liberation Front spokesperson.

Quoted in Steve Hymon, "Animal Rights Leader Justifies Violence," *Los Angeles Times*, November 13, 2005, p. B3.

What made the campaign against HLS most notable, however, was that SHAC did not limit their activities to Huntingdon facilities and staff members. SHAC also engaged in "tertiary targeting" by taking aim at companies that had business ties to HLS in an attempt to drive it out of business. For example, a smoke

One of the longterm targets of the animal rights' radical fringe was Huntingdon Life Sciences (HLS), a company that conducts product safety tests on animals.

bomb exploded inside the Seattle office of a company that sold insurance to HLS. Employees of that company were harassed at home through late-night phone calls, threatening e-mails, people going through their mail, and protesters gathering outside their homes shouting and banging drums.

Perhaps most disturbing to victims was SHAC's practice of posting the names and home addresses of Huntingdon employees and their business associates—and even listing the after-school activities of their children—on their Web site. The site also featured "terror tactic" suggestions and kept a tally of attacks. This approach proved successful. Dozens of companies doing business with HLS, from accounting firms to their landscapers, submitted to the harassment and ended their relationships with the company.

Eventually, six SHAC activists—including its president, campaign coordinator, and Web site coordinator—were arrested and convicted of conspiracy and stalking. In 2006 they received sentences of four to six years in prison, and SHAC was fined $1 million. This case attracted international attention because it was the first prosecution under the U.S. Animal Enterprise Protection Act, enacted in 1992. This law made it a crime to cause any "physical disruption" to animal research labs or other lawful animal-related businesses. In 2006 the law was strengthened to also make it a crime to threaten the staff of animal-related businesses or their family members as well as any companies or individuals with whom they do business. The new law was titled the Animal Enterprise Terrorism Act.

Protesters support the Stop Huntingdon Animal Cruelty (SHAC) group members on trial for terrorism, conspiracy, and attacks against Huntingdon Life Sciences businesses and workers in 2006.

This law has been greeted with dismay by animal rights activists. "That's just a sad commentary, when people killing animals are calling other people terrorists,"[87] scoffs Camille Hankins of the North American Animal Liberation Press Office. Others express concern that the new law broadly targets the rights of free speech. "The [law] sends a chilling message to activists of all social movements that political opportunists can use the rhetoric and resources of the War on Terrorism against them. . . . Anyone paying attention would see clear as day that the legislation was meant to have a chilling effect on all dissent,"[88] says Will Potter, writing about the passage of the Animal Enterprise Terrorism Act in *Earth First!* magazine.

Cursed by Radicals

"Just as the pro-life movement is haunted by the murderers of abortion doctors, the environmental and animal-rights movements are cursed by their own packs of fierce radicals." —John J. Miller, political reporter for the *National Review*

John J. Miller, "In the Name of Animals," *National Review*, July 3, 2006, p. 38.

The new law will probably not deter animal rights extremists already committing illegal acts. One supporter of the convicted SHAC activists responded to the sentencing by saying, "It's sad for all of us to see our friends go to prison, but at the end of the day, it's six individuals, and there are hundreds, thousands of people campaigning against Huntingdon."[89]

Bridging the Gap

As with many controversial issues, there are no clear solutions to bridging the widening gulf of viewpoints between supporters and critics of the animal rights movement. Animal rights advocate Michael Tobias acknowledges the range of opinions that exist on the subject. "It is fair, and necessary, to acknowledge myriad grays in between the worlds of meat eating and vegetarianism, between those who would demand no human being ever exploit any animal . . . and those who find such points-of-view to be extreme or, at the very least, impractical,"[90] he says.

Showdown at Sea

Since 1977 the Sea Shepherd Conservation Society has focused on using extreme tactics in their campaign to protect marine wildlife. One of Sea Shepherd's stated missions is enforcing the whaling moratorium enacted by the International Whaling Commission. Sea Shepherd uses direct action to investigate, document, and sometimes interfere with what they say are the illegal whaling activities of Norway, Iceland, and Japan. Over the past thirty years Sea Shepherd has interfered with whaling fleets by chasing and ramming their ships, attacking them with smoke bombs, tangling their propellers, and even sinking whaling vessels in port.

More mainstream marine conservation groups consider Sea Shepherd's tactics extreme, suggesting that these methods endanger human lives and may actually harm their cause by angering governments and alienating the public. Sea Shepherd counters that their mission is the protection of the marine environment at whatever cost necessary. The organization considers its role vital for enforcing international laws and treaties on the high seas where no law enforcement exists. While no one has yet been injured in Sea Shepherd activities, the organization has endured arrests and seizure of Sea Shepherd ships. Regardless of the setbacks and criticism, Sea Shepherd president Paul Watson insists their work will continue: "Killing highly endangered species in a whale Sanctuary in violation of a global moratorium on commercial whaling are crimes. Trying to stop this insanity through non-violent tactics is simply attempting to uphold the rule of law against criminal actions."

Paul Watson, "Taking on the Goliath of Doom from the Land of the Rising Sun," Sea Shepherd Conservation Society Web site commentary, November 15, 2007. www.seashepherd.org/editorials/editorial_071115_1.html.

Crewmen onboard the Robert Hunter inspect damage to the ship after it collided with a Japanese whaling ship in 2007.

Deborah Rudacille, a former researcher at the Johns Hopkins Center for Alternatives to Animal Testing, proposes that despite their conflicting viewpoints concerning the treatment of animals, people on both sides of the issue must ultimately respect each individual's opinion on the matter:

> The very fact that we are able to entertain these questions at all points to a key difference between human beings and other animals. Whether that difference is profound enough to enable us to continue to use animals as food, as experimental subjects, as the means to our ends, is something that each of us must contemplate and decide in the private space of individual conscience—recognizing that our answer to that question may well conflict with those of other people of good will and conscience. This ambiguous and unsettling outcome may be the best that we can hope for until our unquenchable human ingenuity finds a path beyond the conflict and a solution to which all can, in good conscience, agree.[91]

NOTES

Introduction: The Role of Animals

1. Quoted in "Overview of the Historical Materials," Michigan State University College of Law, Animal Legal and Historical Center. www.animallaw.info/historical/articles/ovushistory.htm#The%20British%20Set%20the%20Stage.

Chapter 1: Should Animals Have Rights?

2. Gary L. Francione, *Introduction to Animal Rights: Your Child or the Dog?* Philadelphia: Temple University Press, 2000, p. xxv.
3. Francione, *Introduction to Animal Rights*, p. xxix.
4. Mark Bekoff, *Strolling with Our Kin.* Jenkintown, PA: Anti-Vivisection Society, 2000, p. 29.
5. Francione, *Introduction to Animal Rights*, p. xxxiv.
6. Quoted in Richard Ryder, "Discrimination on the Basis of Species is Unjust," *The Rights of Animals.* San Diego: Greenhaven, 1999, p. 25.
7. Quoted in L. Neil Smith, "Animals Are the Property of Humans," *The Rights of Animals.* San Diego: Greenhaven, 1999, p. 38.
8. Quoted in R.G. Frey, "Animal Life Is Less Valuable than Human Life," *The Rights of Animals.* San Diego: Greenhaven, 1999, p. 33.
9. Quoted in Matthew Scully, *Dominion.* New York: St. Martin's, 2002, p. 6.
10. Mark Bekoff, *The Emotional Lives of Animals.* Novato, CA: New World Library, 2007, p. 134.
11. Francione, *Introduction to Animal Rights*, p. 141.
12. Peter Singer, *Animal Liberation.* New York: New York Review, 1975, p. 19.
13. Jane Goodall, foreword to *The Emotional Lives of Animals*, p. xiii.
14. Leland Shapiro, *Applied Animal Ethics.* New York: Delmar Thomson Learning, 2000, p. 153.
15. Shapiro, *Applied Animal Ethics*, p. 154.
16. Richard A. Epstein, "The Next Rights Revolution?" *National Review*, November 8, 1999. http://findarticles.com/p/articles/mi_m1282/is_21_51/ai_56899764.

17. Quoted in Daniel T. Oliver, *Animal Rights: The Inhumane Crusade.* Bellevue, WA: Capital Research Center, 1999, p. xiv.
18. Quoted in Ryder, "Discrimination on the Basis of Species Is Unjust," p. 26.

Chapter 2: Farming Animals for Food

19. Shapiro, *Applied Animal Ethics*, p. 188.
20. Richard W. Bulliet, *Hunters, Herders, and Hamburgers.* New York: Columbia University Press, 2005, p. 3.
21. Francione, *Introduction to Animal Rights*, p. xxi.
22. James Serpell, *In the Company of Animals.* New York: Basil Blackwell, 1986, pp. 15–16.
23. Gaverick Matheny and Kai M.A. Chan, "Human Diets and Animal Welfare: The Illogic of the Larder," *Journal of Agricultural and Environmental Ethics*, 2005, vol. 18, pp. 581–82.
24. Shapiro, *Applied Animal Ethics*, p. 172.
25. Quoted in Joby Warrick, "They Die Piece by Piece," *Washington Post*, April 10, 2001, p. A1.
26. Quoted in Warrick, "They Die Piece by Piece," p. A1.
27. Temple Grandin, "Progress and Challenges in Animal Handling and Slaughter in the U.S.," *Applied Animal Behavior Science*, 2006, pp. 129–39. www.grandin.com/references/progress.challenges.us.animal.handling.html.
28. Bryan Salvage, "Revolutionizing the Veal Industry," *Meat Processing*, December 2006, p. 15.
29. Alexei Barrionuevo, "Pork Producer Says It Plans to Give Pigs More Room," *New York Times*, January 25, 2007. www.nytimes.com/2007/01/26/business/26pigs.html.
30. Barrionuevo, "Pork Producer Says It Plans to Give Pigs More Room."
31. Marc Kaufman, "Largest Pork Processor to Phase Out Crates," *Washington Post*, January 26, 2007, p. A6.
32. Francione, *Introduction to Animal Rights*, p. 188.
33. Paul Vitello, "Being Nice to the Bacon, Before You Bring It Home," *New York Times*, April 1, 2007, p. 4.
34. George F. Will, "What We Owe What We Eat," *Newsweek*, July 18, 2005, p. 66.

Chapter 3: Animal Experimentation

35. C. Ray Greek and Jean Swingle Greek, *Sacred Cows and Golden Geese.* New York: Continuum, 2000, pp. 17–18.
36. Quoted in George Page, *Inside the Animal Mind.* New York: Doubleday, 1999, p. 260.

37. American Medical Association, "Use of Animals in Biomedical Research." In Leland Shapiro, *Applied Animal Ethics*. New York: Delmar, 2000, p. A22.

Chapter 4: Animals in Sport and Entertainment

38. Quoted in Tracy Wilkinson, "Rebirth in the Arena," *Los Angeles Times*, October 16, 2007, p. A1.
39. Quoted in Wilkinson, "Rebirth in the Arena," p. A1.
40. Quoted in Warren St. John, "Bullfights? Your Club or Mine?" *New York Times*, December 11, 2005, p. 9.1.
41. Quoted in Dan Bilefsky, "Matador Wins. Bull Dies. The End? Not in Portugal," *New York Times*, August 12, 2007, p. A10.
42. Quoted in Bilefsky, "Matador Wins. Bull Dies. The End? Not in Portugal."
43. Quoted in Diego Cevallos, "Mexico: Bullfighting—Historic Spectacle or Brutal Savagery?" *Global Information Network*, February 9, 2006, p. 1.
44. Quoted in Peter Whoriskey, "Cockfighting on the Web Enters Legal Arena," *Washington Post*, July 22, 2007, p. A3.
45. Quoted in Rebecca Meiser, "Chicken Wars," *Cleveland Scene*, July 4, 2007.
46. Quoted in Jack Douglas Jr., "Texas Slaying Puts Spotlight on World of Illegal Dogfights," *Seattle Times*, September 2, 2006, p. A3.
47. Quoted in Paul Duggan, "A Blood Sport Exposed," *Washington Post*, August 22, 2007, p. A1.
48. Quoted in Larry Silver, "Activists Protest Animal Treatment; Rodeo Defends Actions," *Arizona Daily Star*, February 28, 2004. www.fox11az.com/news/local/stories/022804ccktFOX11Rodeo.3a729a44.html#.
49. Quoted in George Vecsey, "Sports of the Times; Racing Can't Afford More Tragedies," *New York Times*, June 6, 1993. http://query.nytimes.com/gst/fullpage.html?res=9F0CE7D81E3DF935A35755C0A965958260.
50. Quoted in George Vecsey, "Psychic Pull of an Injured Racehorse," *New York Times*, May 24, 2006. http://select.nytimes.com/2006/05/24/sports/othersports/24vecsey.html.
51. Quoted in Karyn Hunt, "Spurred by Animal Abuse, Local Officials Reshaping the Big Top," *Los Angeles Times*, November 2, 1997, p. 6.
52. Quoted in Hunt, "Spurred by Animal Abuse, Local Officials Reshaping the Big Top," p. 6.

Chapter 5: Animal Rights and Wildlife

53. Bulliet, *Hunters, Herders, and Hamburgers*, p. 62.

54. People for the Ethical Treatment of Animals Fact Sheet, *Why Sport Hunting is Cruel and Unnecessary*. www.helpinganimals.com/Factsheet/files/FactsheetDisplay.asp?ID=53.
55. Quoted in Scully, *Dominion*. p. 107.
56. Quoted in Jim Robbins, "Under Growing Criticism, Hunters Discuss Ethics to Restore Their Image," *New York Times*, September 15, 1996. http://query.nytimes.com/gst/fullpage.html?res=9E01E0D9153AF936A2575AC0A960958260&sec=&spon=&pagewanted=print.
57. National Rifle Association, "The Hunter's Image." www.nrahq.org/hunting/hunterimage.asp.
58. Quoted in Steve Tuttle, "The Elusive Hunter," *Newsweek*, December 4, 2006. www.newsweek.com/id/43951/.
59. Quoted in Tuttle, "The Elusive Hunter."
60. Quoted in James A. Swan, *In Defense of Hunting*. San Francisco: HarperSanFrancisco, 1995, p. 12.
61. Quoted in Michael Satchell, "A View to a Kill," Humane Society of the United States. www.hsus.org/archive/about_us/about_hsus_programs_and_services/eye_on_the_opposition/a_view_to_a_kill_how_safari_club_intl_works_to_weaken_esa_protections.html.
62. Quoted in Satchell, "A View to a Kill."
63. Quoted in Humane Society of the United States, "Unfair Chase: Ethical Objections from Both Ends of the Spectrum." www.hsus.org/hunt/campaigns/canned/ethical_objections.html.
64. Quoted in Am Johal, "Canada: Activists Protest Hunters' Plan to Kill 270,000 seals," *Global Information Network*, April 5, 2007, p. 1.
65. Quoted in Sea Shepherd Conservation Society, "Seal Hunt Facts." www.seashepherd.org/seals/seals_seal_hunt_facts.html.
66. Quoted in Douglas Belkin, "Seal Hunters Fight Long Cruelty Label," *Wall Street Journal*, March 23, 2007, p. B3.
67. The Institute of Cetacean Research, "Japan's Research Whaling in the Arctic." www.icrwhale.org/QandAResearch.htm.
68. Greenpeace, "Whaling 101." www.greenpeace.org/usa/campaigns/oceans/whale-defenders/whaling-101.
69. Quoted in Greenpeace, "Whale Defenders." www.greenpeace.org/usa/campaigns/oceans/whale-defenders.

Chapter 6: The Tactics of Animal Rights Activists: Do They Go Too Far?

70. Wesley J. Smith, "Four Legs Good, Two Legs Bad: The Anti-Human Values of 'Animal Rights,'" *Human Life Review*, Winter 2007, p. 8.
71. Quoted in Smith, "Four Legs Good, Two Legs Bad," p. 9.

72. Quoted in Shapiro, *Applied Animal Ethics*, p. 310.
73. Quoted in Alex Epstein, "The 'Animal Rights' Movement's Cruelty to Human Well-Being," *New York Beacon*, August 25–31, 2005, p. 23.
74. Daniel T. Oliver, *Animal Rights*, p. 104.
75. Quoted in Zenitha Prince, "PETA Generates Outrage; Equating Blacks with Mistreated Animals," *Afro-American*, August 27–September 2, 2005, p. A1.
76. Quoted in Smith, "Four Legs Good, Two Legs Bad," p. 13.
77. Quoted in Prince, "PETA Generates Outrage; Equating Blacks with Mistreated Animals," p. A1.
78. Quoted in Prince, "PETA Generates Outrage; Equating Blacks with Mistreated Animals," p. A1.
79. Quoted in Prince, "PETA Generates Outrage; Equating Blacks with Mistreated Animals," p. A1.
80. Animal Liberation Front, "The ALF Credo and Guidelines." http://animalliberationfront.com/ALFront/alf_credo.htm.
81. Quoted in Smith, "Four Legs Good, Two Legs Bad," p. 13.
82. Quoted in Gloria Kim, "Saving Animals, They Hunt Humans," *Maclean's*, March 20, 2006, p. 38.
83. Quoted in Rebecca Trounson and Joe Mozingo, "UCLA to Protect Animal Research," *Los Angeles Times*, August 26, 2006, p A1.
84. Quoted in Joe Mozingo, "A Thin Line on Animal Rights," *Los Angeles Times*, September 5, 2006, p. B1.
85. Quoted in Steve Hymon, "Animal Rights Leader Justifies Violence," *Los Angeles Times*, November 13, 2005, p. B3.
86. Quoted in Mozingo, "A Thin Line on Animal Rights," p. B1.
87. Quoted in Trounson and Mozingo, "UCLA to Protect Animal Research," p A1.
88. Will Potter, "Animal Enterprise Terrorism Act Signed into Law," *Earth First!* January/February 2007, p.8.
89. Quoted in Laura Mansnerus, "Animal Rights Advocates Given Prison Terms," *New York Times*, September 13, 2006, p. B8.
90. Michael Tobias, *Voices from the Underground*. Pasadena, CA: New Paradigm, 1999, p. 27.
91. Deborah Rudacille, *The Scalpel and the Butterfly: The War Between Animal Research and Animal Protection*. New York: Farrar, Straus and Giroux, 2000, pp. 312–13.

Discussion Questions

Chapter 1: Should Animals Have Rights?
1. Explain the difference between animal welfare and animal rights.
2. How does Mark Bekoff's statement that "well-being centers on what animals feel, not what they know" relate to the suffering of animals?
3. Should certain types of animals, such as dogs or primates, be granted more rights than other types of animals, such as chickens or rats? Why or why not?

Chapter 2: Farming Animals for Food
1. Does the need to produce inexpensive and abundant food justify the conditions of animals raised on factory farms?
2. What does Gary Francione mean by the term "moral schizophrenia"?
3. What are some of the forces that could lead to the improved treatment of meat animals?

Chapter 3: Animal Experimentation
1. How have people benefited from the use of animals in medical research?
2. Should students be required to dissect animals in the classroom? Why or why not?
3. How does the set of guiding principles known as the Three R's govern the treatment of laboratory animals?

Chapter 4: Animals in Sport and Entertainment
1. Is cruelty to animals justified for the sake of maintaining cultural traditions? Why or why not?

2. Why do illegal blood sports such as dogfighting and cockfighting continue to be practiced in the United States?

3. Do you think people who use animals for sports such as rodeo or horse racing are concerned for their welfare? Explain your answer.

Chapter 5: Animal Rights and Wildlife

1. Why is hunting more controversial now than it was one hundred years ago?

2. How does hunting contribute to wildlife conservation?

3. Is it OK to hunt some wild animals but not others? Explain your answer.

Chapter 6: The Tactics of Animal Rights Activists: Do They Go Too Far?

1. Are animal rights organizations up front about their motives? If so, why? If not, why not?

2. Why do some animal rights organizations deliberately design campaigns to cause controversy?

3. Should extreme animal rights activists who engage in illegal activities be considered terrorists? Why or why not?

ORGANIZATIONS TO CONTACT

American Anti-Vivisection Society (AAVS)
801 Old York Rd., #204
Jenkintown, PA 19046
Phone: (215) 887-0816
Web site: www.aavs.org

The AAVS opposes experiments on living animals and promotes alternative research methods. The organization produces videos, magazines, and brochures, including the *Compassionate Shopping Guide*.

American Association for Laboratory Animal Science (AALAS)
9190 Crestwyn Hills Dr.
Memphis, TN 38125
Phone: (901) 754-8620
Web site: www.aalas.org

The AALAS is a professional organization devoted to the care and study of animals used in medical research. It provides seminars and publications for lab animal technicians as well as a technician-certification program.

Animal Welfare Institute (AWI)
PO Box 3650
Washington, DC 20027
Phone: (703) 836-4300
Web site: www.animalwelfare.com

AWI works to reduce the suffering of animals used in agriculture and research. It also campaigns against fur trapping and for protection of wildlife.

Humane Society of the United States (HSUS)
2100 L St., NW
Washington, DC 20037
Phone: (202) 452-1100
Web site: www.hsus.org

Established in 1954, the HSUS is the country's largest animal protection organization. Its programs cover a wide variety of animal issues, including promoting the humane treatment of animals in agriculture and research.

People for the Ethical Treatment of Animals (PETA)
501 Front St.
Norfolk, VA 23510
Phone: (757) 622-7382
Web site: www.peta.org

PETA claims to be the world's largest animal rights organization. PETA uses public education, cruelty investigations, legislation, celebrity involvement, and protest campaigns to bring attention to the uses of animals on factory farms, in laboratories, in the clothing trade, and in the entertainment industry.

Books

Tamara L. Roleff, ed., *Current Controversies: The Rights of Animals.* San Diego, CA: Greenhaven, 1999. A balanced look at both sides of the issues of animal rights, hunting, animal experimentation, food animals, and animals in entertainment.

Lisa Trumbauer, *Exploring Animal Rights and Animal Welfare.* Westport, CT: Middle School Reference, 2002. A four-volume set examining the ways animals are treated by people. Includes volumes on using animals for food, research, clothing, and entertainment.

Kelly Wand, ed., *American Social Movements: Animal Rights.* San Diego, CA: Greenhaven, 2002. A collection of essays, speeches, book excerpts, and personal comments provide a historical overview of the animal rights movement.

Web Sites

American Association for Laboratory Animal Science Fact Sheet, *Use of Animals in Biomedical Research: Understanding the Issues* (www.aalas.org/pdf/08-00007.pdf). An overview of the benefits of using animals in research. The article also contains links for more information.

Americans for Medical Progress (www.amprogress.org). This organization provides information on the use of animals in medical research. The site also provides counterpoints to claims made by animal rights organizations against animal research.

Animal Legal and Historical Center, Michigan State University College of Law (www.animallaw.info). This comprehensive site contains a catalog of laws and legal cases relating to animals in the United States and around the world. Visitors can search for laws by topic, animal species, state, or country.

Humane Farming Association (www.hfa.org). This organization is dedicated to reducing cruelty to farm animals and ending the practice of factory farming.

In Defense of Animals (www.idausa.org). In Defense of Animals campaigns against animal abuse and cruelty and advocates for ending the property status of animals.

Library Index, "Animals in Sports: Major Animal Sports and Their Controversies" (www.libraryindex.com/pages/2188/Animals-in-Sports-MAJOR-ANIMAL-SPORTS-ANDTHEIR-CONTROVERSIES.html). A comprehensive overview of the use of animals in sports, including numerous statistics.

National Rifle Association (www.nra.org). The National Rifle Association advocates for the rights of hunters and provides hunter education and safety training.

INDEX

A
Actors, animal, 67
Aldworth, Rebecca, 87
American Medical Association (AMA), on use of animals in research, 55–56
American Society for the Prevention of Cruelty to Animals (ASPCA), 9
Americans for Medical Progress, 55
Animal Enterprise Protection Act (1992), 102
Animal Enterprise Terrorism Act (2006), 102–103
Animal Farm (Orwell), 30
Animal Liberation campaign, 95–96
Animal Liberation Front (ALF), 94, 97–100
Animal Libertion (Singer), 20
Animal rights
   animal welfare vs., 11, 13
   law school courses on, 23
Animal Rights: The Inhumane Crusade (Oliver), 15–16, 94
Animal rights movement
   birth of, 13–15
   concern over tactics of, 91–105
Animal Welfare Act (AWA, 1966), 51, 53
   facts about, 52
Animals
   early organizations promoting humane treatment of, 9–10
   evolving relationship between humans and, 6–7
   numbers killed in hunting, 76
   numbers slaughtered for food, 25
Anticruelty laws, 10–11
Association of Zoos and Aquariums, 58

B
Barbaro (thoroughbred colt), 69
Barker, Bob, 23
Bearbaiting/bullbaiting, 58–59
Behavioral research, 41
Bekoff, Mark, 15, 39, 53
Bible, 6
Blood sports, 57–59
Bullfighting, 59–61
Bulliet, Richard, 27
Burros, Marian, 36

C
Carpio, Isabel, 60
Carr, Dawn, 96
Chan, Kai, 30
Chickens
   factory farming of, 29–30
   slaughter of, 37
   See also Cockfighting
CHIMP (Chimpanzee Health Improvement, Maintenance, and Protection) Act (2000), 49
Circuses, 72–73
Clinton, Bill, 49
Cockfighting, 61–63
Confinement pens, 36
Consciousness, animal vs. human, 17–20
Cruelty to Animals Act (England, 1835), 59

D
DeRose, Chris, 93
Dogfighting, 63–66
Dogs, use in research, 41–42
Dolphins, hunting of, 90

E
Education, use of animals for dissection in, 48
Egg production, 29
   cage-free, 35–36
Epstein, Alex, 92
Equal consideration, principle of, 13

117

F

Factory farms, 25–26, 28–30
  benefits of, 30, 32
Fast food chains, improvement in food animal production and, 34–36
Fearing, Jennifer, 21
Fish, perception of pain by, 80
Fixed Dose Procedure, 43
Fois gras, 31
Food, number of animals slaughtered for, 25
Foxhunting, 84
Francione, Gary, 13, 25, 27–28, 39
Friedlander, Lester, 33
Fur, for fashion industry, 83, 85–87

G

Galvin, Joan, 73
Genetic engineering, 47
Goodall, Jane, 19–20, 51
Grandin, Temple, 34–35
Great Ape Project, 12
Greek, Jean, 46–47
Greek, Ray, 46–47
Greenpeace, 88, 89
Greyhound Protection League, 71
Greyhound racing, 71

H

Hall, H. Dale, 79
Hankins, Camille, 103
Holocaust on Your Plate campaign, 95
Horse racing, 69–70, 72
Horses, slaughter of, 37
Humane Index, 21
Humane Slaughter Act (1958), 33, 34
  exemption of poultry from, 37
Humane Society of the United States (HSUS), 21, 63, 65, 87
Hunting, 74–76
  decline in, 79–80
  fox, 84
  role in conservation, 77–79
  seal, 85–87
  trophy, 81–83
  whale, 87–90
Huntingdon Life Sciences (HLS), 100–101

I

In the Company of Animals (Serpell), 11, 28
In Defense of Hunting (Swan), 75
Institute of Cetacean Research, 88–89
Institutional Animal Care and Use Committees (IACUC), 51, 53
International Whaling Commission (IWC), 87

J

Jackson, John J., Jr., 82
Jones, Terry, 96

K

Knox, Margaret, 75

L

Lethal Dose 50 (LD-50) test, 43
Levey, Colin, 64
London, Edythe, 94

M

Marino, Lori, 90
Martin, Jonathan, 63
Matheny, Gaverick, 30
Meat production
  people ignore reality of, 26–27
  See also Factory farms
Miller, John J., 13
Moral schizophrenia, 27–28
Morality
  of animal rights, 20–21
  humane treatment of animals is based on, 15–16
Moutinho, Miguel, 61

N

National Association of Colored People (NAACP), 96
National Rifle Association (NRA), 78, 79
Newkirk, Ingrid, 92, 93

O

Oliver, Daniel T., 15–16, 94
Opinion polls. *See* Surveys
Orwell, George, 30

P

Pacelle, Wayne, 36–37, 63
Paul, Ron, 39
People for the Ethical Treatment of Animals (PETA), 22, 67, 81, 91
  concern over tactics of, 92–93, 95–96
  on hunting, 75

Pets, 28
Philips, Trevor, 41
Pigs/sows
    factory farming of, 30
    use in research, 41–42
Polls. *See* Surveys
Posewitz, Jim, 79, 83
Potter, Will, 103
Primates, use in research, 24, 48, 50–51
    defense of, 94
Primatt, Humphrey, 7
Professional Rodeo Cowboys Association (PRCA), 67, 68
Puck, Wolfgang, 31

R
Regan, Tom, 22–23, 96
Reiss, Diana, 90
Research, animal, 40
    alternatives to, 55–56
    criticism of using animals as human models, 46–48
    defense of, 94
    in drug testing/product safety, 43, 44–46
    in genetic engineering, 47
    medical advances from, 41
    opposition to, 43–44
    as target of animal rights activists, 97–102
    use of primates in, 24, 48, 50–51
Rhodes, Amy, 69
Rodents, use in research, 42–43
Rodeo, 66–69
Rowe, Claudia, 68
Rudacille, Deborah, 105
Ryder, Richard, 16, 24

S
Sabin, Heloisa, 55
Safari Club International (SCI), 81–82
Sarinato, Richard, 73
Sato, Junichi, 89
Scully, Matthew, 44
Scully, Ron, 39
Sea Shepherd Conservation Society, 104
Serpell, James, 11, 28

Singer, Peter, 19, 20
Slaughterhouses
    fast food chain monitoring of, 34–35
    kosher/halal, 34
    violations of animal welfare at, 33
Smith, L. Neil, 17
Smith, Wesley J., 91, 98
Smithfield Farms, 36
Society for the Prevention of Cruelty to Animals (SPCA), 9
Speciesism, 16, 20
Stewart, Bill, 66
Stop Huntingdon Animal Cruelty (SHAC), 100–102
Strauss, Randy, 36
Strauss Veal, 36
Surveys
    on hunting, 80
    on support for animal rights/welfare, 23
Swan, James A., 75

T
Three Rs guidelines, 53–54
Tobias, Michael, 103
Trapping, 83, 85
Treacy, Dennis, 36

V
Veal production, 30
    improvements in animal welfare in, 36
Vecsey, George, 70
Vegetarianism, benefits of, 38–39
Vitello, Peter, 27

W
Wallace, George N., 75
Walsh, Ed, 98
Watson, Paul, 87, 104
Whaling, 87–90
Whoriskey, Peter, 59
Wildlife management, role of hunting in, 77

Z
Zoos, controversy over role of, 58

PICTURE CREDITS

Cover: Image copyright Anita, 2008. Used under license from Shutterstock.com
AFP/Getty Images, 38
AP Images, 7, 10, 12, 14, 19, 22, 26, 29, 31, 35, 49, 54, 56, 60, 62, 65, 66, 70, 71, 76, 78, 82, 84, 85, 88, 93, 101, 102, 104
Tim Boyle/Getty Images, 72
John E. Fletcher/National Geographic/Getty Images, 42
Fritz Goro/Time & Life Pictures/Getty Images, 45
Chris Holmes/Time & Life Pictures/Getty Images, 97
Philippe Psaila/Photo Researchers, Inc., 17
© José Fuste Raga/zefa/Corbis, 32
Steve Winter/National Geographic/Getty Images, 50
Steve Zmina, 52

ABOUT THE AUTHOR

Karen D. Povey has spent her career as a conservation educator, working to instill an appreciation for wildlife and wild places in people of all ages. Karen makes her home in Gig Harbor, Washington, and presents live animal programs at Tacoma's Point Defiance Zoo and Aquarium. She has written many books on wildlife and the environment, including *Leopards, The Condor, Life in a Swamp*, and *Energy Alternatives*.